THE TEETH GROW SHARPER STILL

K.M.Bishop

—Shellville Press—

Printed by Shellville Press in the United States of America

Cover illustration by Natalie Qualmann, @nats.mcgats

ISBN: 978-1-7334487-8-9

Shellville Press
a division of Shellville Design LLC
www.shellvillepress.com

10 9 8 7 6 5 4 3 2 1

Also by K.M.Bishop:

The Nameless

The Prophet

My Dear Margaret

PREFACE

The beast watched the young woman from the darkness; its teeth bared into a blood-thirsty smile. Was this to be its next victim? It watched from the top of the hill as the young woman walked along the familiar path, one the beast knew she had taken many times; it had smelled her before.

The beast moved quickly and silently, parallel to the woman as it tried to stay out of what light the full moon gave off. Ah! The full moon. The time when the beast had the most strength. The time when the beast's hunger took control.

The woman stopped a moment and bent over, messing with the hem of her dress. The beast almost laughed. If it happened now—no, it could not happen now. It would be too easy; it wouldn't be as fun. No, just a little longer. Half of the fun was the stalking, the chase.

The beast waited patiently for the woman to continue, all the time salivating at the thought of what was to come; its long tongue smacked at its lips, remembering the others, imagining the warmth of her blood as it flowed from her; the metallic smell and taste engulfing it, seducing it. It could not wait, yet, it had to. Patience meant assurance, and it would *not be long now.*

Finally, the woman began walking again, and the beast began with her, mimicking her, making sure its steps were hers; both hitting the ground at the same time.

Just a few more moments, it thought. We will be there in just a few moments.

Patience was beginning to give way as the animalistic desire to chase coursed through the beast's veins giving it energy, giving it life. Its heart raced as it saw the bend in the road, the opening to the valley and it had to pause a moment to recollect itself for the urge to howl and alert its prey to its presence was almost overwhelming.

The beast quickened its pace, gaining lightly on the woman. Its heart pounded so loudly, it was almost afraid it would alarm the woman to her stalker, but the woman was clueless; lost in her dreams of the future, no doubt.

Oh, how the beast wished it could laugh! Dreaming about a future that would never come!

This is it, the beast thought excitedly. We are finally here.

Without waiting another moment, the beast broke into a sprint, letting its animalistic nature take over.

The woman was fifty yards away.

Twenty-five.

Fifteen. She finally turned around, hearing the beast's approach, but it was too late. Her throat was already in its grasp; her blood was already flowing from her into the beast's mouth. A cold, unfeeling snarl was the last thing she heard as her life slipped away.

"Dr. Greystone, I do not like this story!" said the little boy, with a deep-set frown on his face. "It is scary. Why should you tell a scary story?"

The young girl next to him shook her head and sighed. "It is not a real, Thomas!" she told him impatiently. "If it is not real, what should you have to be afraid of?"

"You are quite right, Aggy," Dr. Alfred Greystone applauded. "Do not fear, Master Thomas. Though it might seem strange things happen on a full moon, Lycans are a thing of myth."

The little boy shifted in his seat. "My grandmama says she remembers a tale about a werewolf in a village close to hers when she was growing up!" Thomas pointed out, still frowning. "She said it plagued their village for years because they could not find the beast."

"Ah, I am sure your grandmama is not lying about a tale of a werewolf," Dr. Greystone began, "but I am also sure if it had been properly investigated, a reasonable explanation could have been found."

He shook his head defiantly. "No, it *was* a werewolf!" he urged. "Grandmama even said she heard her papa talking to some of the concerned villagers one evening. She told me they spoke of a beast so devilish it could only be brought upon this earth by the devil himself and could only be hidden by those who are his minions! Witches, to be exact!"

The little girl pressed a hand to her mouth to stifle a laugh.

The boy glared at her. "Do not laugh, Aggy!" he ordered scoldingly in his little lordly tone. "I am not lying."

"If you are not, then your grandmama surely was! Witches and werewolves to be sure!" The little girl shook her head. "What your father must think of your education if you are to believe such stories! You shall put my uncle to shame!"

Dr. Greystone cleared his throat and raised a reproachful eyebrow at his niece. She sat still at once, refraining from her teasing, but not in the least ashamed of what she had already said.

"Master Thomas, I am sure your grandmother told a wonderful tale of witches and werewolves to make half the country believers and with respect to her station in life, we shall be obliged to understand that the villagers from where she grew up truly believed they had a beast much like a werewolf amongst them." With that, Dr. Greystone gave a half bow to the boy and changed the subject.

The boy, however, pouted the rest of the lesson, refusing to add any more to the conversation and was relieved when it was time for him to return home.

"Thomas does not show much promise, uncle," the young girl sighed when he was gone. "He is nearly eleven and cannot tell the difference between what is real and what is made up!"

Dr. Greystone chuckled. "Yes, child, well, we cannot all be blessed with a lack of imagination as you are."

The girl lifted her brow at her uncle. "You are laughing at me," she pointed out.

Her uncle kissed her on the forehead. "No, my dear," he told her. "I am rather proud of how clever you are; I just sometimes wish you behaved more like your tender age of nine. You are more serious than some of the adults I know."

The young girl regarded her uncle for a moment. "I do not have time for children's games, uncle," she finally replied. "If I am to be as smart as you, I have to dedicate myself to my studies!"

Dr. Greystone beamed at his niece though his heart ached at the same time. He often wondered if his brother would approve of how he was raising his daughter. But then he had to remind himself that his brother was dead, and it did not signify worrying over what the dead might think.

Perhaps if he had remarried, it would have been different.

He would not have had to worry so much since his niece would have had the benefit of a female influence. But that was not to be, so he would have to continue to raise her as best as he knew how, the only way he could. Through logic and academia.

1

1792 (13 YEARS LATER)

Agrippina Greystone stood proudly at the back of her uncle's classroom, waiting for him to finish his lecture. She browsed the young men in the room, counting that maybe only about half were actually paying attention and only half of those students were actually taking notes.

She sighed, discontented with the scene. How rich, young men take for granted their privilege to good education. She wished they all had the good sense to realize how lucky they were to be sitting there learning from one of the greatest minds in Britain, but what do young minds care for except to throw away their advantages and complain later of wasted opportunities?

There was a rumble of noise as the young men stood from their seats, eager to move on to their next class or take a break from the day's studies. They all bowed their heads at her and muttered a greeting as they passed. All of them used to seeing her by now.

She bent over a moment to brush a wrinkle from her

modest dress, causing her almond-colored hair, only done up half of the way, to tumble over her shoulders. She stood and swept it back, a motion that caught the attention of some of the young men walking by, their stares lingering.

"Miss Greystone," came the grinning voice of one of the young men.

"Richard Maddox," she replied less enthused than him, her grey eyes slightly narrowed.

"You are looking remarkably well this afternoon," he told her.

"And you are looking rather the same," she said blandly.

He chuckled. "Come now, old girl, there is no need for that."

Agrippina tried not to sigh. "For what? Obvious observations?" she retorted. "I suppose you are right. Maybe I should lie and tell you how handsome you are and that my knees buckle at the sight of you."

He sucked his teeth, amused. "It certainly would do well for me," he said with a smirk. "A little boost to my ego is surely no consequence to you."

"Forget it, Mr. Maddox," she replied, turning away. "Save your flirtations for a woman dumb enough to be fooled by you."

He laughed. "You are way too pretty, Miss Greystone, to always be this serious. It would not hurt if you smiled every so often, you know?"

She shot him a glance, sizing him up for a moment. "I will smile, Mr. Maddox, when I have something worth smiling about." She gave him a curt nod, and made her way down the stairs to her uncle.

"Ah, good afternoon, my dear!" her uncle exclaimed in greeting.

She smiled affectionately at his appearance. His graying

hair was a little wild, his glasses slightly askew, and chalky handprints littered his dark pants. "The lecture seemed to go well," she told him. "More students appeared to be paying attention this time."

He smiled as he gathered his things. "Yes, it was a rather interesting topic, was it not?" He lifted a playful brow in her direction. "The parallels of Roman and Greek mythology and their effect on today's medicine. I think I should have you write all of my lectures from now on."

Agrippina's frown lines softened for a moment.

"What did Maddox want with you?" he asked as he shoved his notebook and papers into his bag.

"Other than to annoy me? I could not tell you."

Dr. Greystone shouldered his bag. "I think he admires you, you know? I often see him smiling in your direction and when you are not there, he often appears to be awaiting your arrival."

"I am sure he is rather watching the exit and planning his escape."

"Ah, do not doubt your charms, my dear. He smiles and waits for you!"

"Well, he can keep his smiles. The man is an idiot," she declared. "I read his economics paper on supply and demand and he could not understand the correlation between fertilizer prices and its effect on the price of corn."

Her uncle laughed. "I see Professor Hartley has been letting you grade his papers again."

"Yes, well, it gives him more time to spend at the White Lion drowning himself in the bottle," she stated.

"You could do worse than Maddox, Aggy, my dear."

"I do not want to hear it, uncle," she replied urging him out the door. "And I am more convinced I could do ten times better. Regardless of either, I would much prefer a dog."

Her uncle roared in laughter. "Careful, my love, that your bitterness does not consume you. For one day you might find that man who is ten times better than Maddox and then what would you do?"

Aggy looped her arm through the crook of her uncle's. "When that day comes, I am sure I will figure it out."

He gave her a quick peck on her forehead. "Let us go home and see what Abigail has prepared us for lunch. I am rather famished."

"A letter come for you, sir," their maid Abigail said as they entered their house just off of the Cambridge campus. "And lunch is ready n' waitin' in the parlor."

"Thank you, Abigail, that is capital!" Dr. Greystone replied taking the letter she held out for him.

"Where you been walkin', miss?" Abigail asked skeptically, seeing the mud clinging to Agrippina's hem.

"I was grading papers by the river and stepped in a mud puddle," she replied removing her bonnet and handing it to the maid.

Abigail held back a scoff as she took it. "Might you have at least wiped your boots, miss, before you come further into the house? I spent all day cleanin'. At least pretend to care 'bout what I do 'round here."

"Are you not supposed to clean up after me, Abigail?" Agrippina replied in her dry sardonic manner.

Poor Abigail, even after years of working for the Greystones still could never tell when her mistress was joking and when she was being serious, often taking offense when none was meant.

The older woman finally scoffed. "And are you not s'pposed to act a lady being that ya are one?" she replied in a slightly heightened voice.

Agrippina's mouth twitched and she bowed her head a moment to keep from smiling. "You are quite right, Abigail," she gave in. "Neither of us wants to do what we are supposed to." She gave her maid a slight curtsey before removing her boots and leaving them at the door.

"And you better change 'fore you go 'n sit in my clean parlor!" Abigail called after her.

"Did you receive another scolding?" her uncle asked in a teasing tone, putting his letter down once she entered the parlor in a fresh dress.

"If you could believe it," Agrippina replied sitting with a sigh. "We allow her too many liberties sometimes, I believe. Well-bred society might think her too impertinent."

Dr. Greystone chuckled. "Is that not just how we like her?"

"Very true. A common, obsequious servant without complaint would make us think too well of ourselves. An opinionated one is much better for lessons in humility." She placed a few grapes and cheese on her plate.

Again, her uncle laughed. "I know you jest. You think too well of old Abigail to say otherwise."

She gave a subtle smile as she cut her roast beef into small pieces. "I will neither comment as to the truthfulness or falsehood of such a statement." She gestured with her head at the letter. "Anything of interest?"

He glanced down at the letter next to his plate as if he had already forgotten about its contents. "Ah, it is of no consequence. An old friend updating me on his situation in life. Rather dry and unimportant information to anyone who does not know him."

Agrippina lifted a brow at him for a moment, thinking to question him further on the subject, but decided better of it.

Dr. Greystone then burst into a coughing fit, covering his mouth with a handkerchief.

Agrippina gave an unconcerned look in his direction but stood and moved to a small table against the wall and poured him a glass of wine from a decanter stored there. She handed it to him without a word.

He nodded gratefully as he took a sip, and put his handkerchief back into his pocket. "Thank you, my dear," he told her after he regained his voice. "My throat has been rather dry lately. I believe it is all of that chalk dust."

She nodded. "I am sure it is. You should drink more tea with honey while at your office, uncle. It should do away with such fits."

He wagged a finger at her. "I am sure you are right. I will make sure to have a cup every other hour."

They were then interrupted by Abigail hurrying into the room, looking flushed with excitement.

"Oh, miss, ya would not guess!" she proclaimed a little breathlessly.

Agrippina and her uncle blinked at her.

"There is a caller, miss!" she clarified when neither of them ventured to say anything. "A gentleman caller!" She pressed a hand to her cheek. "A handsome gentleman caller!"

"For me?" Agrippina asked in a confused tone, her nose wrinkled.

Abigail nodded. "Only think what this could mean!"

Agrippina shot her uncle a bemused look before standing while he lifted his brows in curious astonishment.

"Well, where is he, Abigail?"

"In the library, miss, for the light is best this time of day. And the sun do fall so lovely on your hair."

"That was very thoughtful of you," Agrippina told her blandly as she moved out of the room.

"Aye, miss, ya know how I am! I am always thinkin' of such things!" she continued as she unnecessarily followed her out of the room. "I am glad you wore this dress. It does bring out the color in yer eyes, miss."

"Thank you, Abigail," Agrippina said sternly turning around. "I am sure I can handle it from here."

"Oh, yes, miss, quite right! How right you are! Oh, just think!" She blushed for her mistress. "How wonderful it is!"

"Dear Abigail, I believe you are assuming more than you should. Please, go and see if my uncle needs anything and leave me to my visitor. I will be quite alright."

The maid flushed again, but was too excited to take any offense. She gave a small curtsey and shuffled back to the parlor.

Agrippina then resumed her way to the library where she paused and took a deep breath before entering.

She balked when she saw who her visitor was.

"Mr. Maddox?"

The gentleman turned and smirked at her before bowing deeply. "Miss Greystone."

"What on earth are you doing here?" she asked in surprise.

"Is your housemaid quite alright?" he inquired, ignoring her question. "I thought she was going to faint when she saw me."

She nodded slowly. "She is quite fine, I thank you, Mr. Maddox," she replied regaining herself. "I thank you."

His smile returned. "My appearance here surprises you." He seemed pleased.

She stood taller. "I was not expecting you, no." She cleared her throat, his unmovable gaze making her uncomfortable. "May I ask to what I owe the pleasure of your visit?"

He chuckled and finally looked away. "It is perhaps a little simpler than what your maid had supposed. The Hills are having a gathering tomorrow night and I want you to go as my guest," Mr. Maddox explained.

"You *want* me to go as your guest?" she repeated a little skeptically. "That seems to be a rather strange way to invite someone. Are you requesting me to go with you or demanding me?"

He smirked. "Politely ordering."

Agrippina raised her brows in surprised annoyance. "I am not sure if your response is a reflection of what you think I want to hear or of your inability to understand how to speak to a lady."

He laughed. "Come now, Miss Greystone! I am trying to make light of the situation. If you do not want to go, I will not force you though I might become vexed. If you do go, however, I shall promise to tease you less."

"That is a lie if ever I heard one. I have known your antics for too long."

He laughed again. "Fine, but I must have you come, if only to see you smile for an evening."

She regarded him for a moment.

"Come, come, Miss Greystone! There will be plenty to entertain you. There will be dancing and card games and good food."

Her features almost lightened into a smile. "Do you dance then?"

"I do," he replied matter-of-factly.

"And, if I went as your guest, you would expect me to dance with you?"

He gave a slow nod, repressing a smile. "Indeed, I would be honored if you would."

"And, my acquiescing would, therefore, give you a reason to touch me, even hold me close to you?"

A faint blush spread over his cheeks. "I have always

admired your bluntness. Some, I am sure, would find it unbecoming in a woman, but I find it rather amusing."

She only lifted a brow in reply, waiting for him to finish answering her question.

Finally, he nodded with a smile. "Within reason, yes, it would give me limited permission to touch you, but within the bounds of propriety only, of course. For you have to admit, it would look rather strange for us to be dancing without touching, would it not?"

"Yes, it would."

"I promise to be the perfect gentleman."

She huffed laughingly. "You act the gentleman? I would never believe it."

"You would if you came for then you would see it, and seeing is believing."

She thought for a moment. "The Hills, you said?"

He nodded.

She took a deep breath and let it out slowly. "I shall think it over and let you know in the morning."

He smiled and bowed. "You shall not regret it and it would bring me and many others pleasure to see you in attendance."

"Many others?" she inquired skeptically.

He nodded. "There are other young men from your uncle's classes whom you will recognize. Would you not wish to surprise them?"

She narrowed her eyes. "Is this some sort of bet? Are you to lose money if I did not come?"

Maddox scoffed, pressing a hand to his chest in an offended manner. "I am hurt you would think that. Honestly, it speaks to your lack of confidence. Is it so silly that a man of the same age as you wishes to spend time in your presence?"

She regarded him for a moment. "Tomorrow, Mr. Maddox," she replied. "I shall let you know tomorrow."

He laughed and gave another bow. "I shall eagerly await your reply." He then happily left the room.

2

Abigail was mildly disappointed Agrippina's visitor only invited her to a gathering, but was soon delighted again at it being a sign of the handsome young man's affections toward her. Agrippina set her straight without wasting another moment.

"Mr. Maddox, were he attached to me, would not succeed in advancing my feelings. He is a shallow man without taste or intelligence above what might be considered average."

Abigail gaped at her. "Miss, if that is your attitude toward every man who walks in the door, I am sure as I am breathing you will die an old maid!"

Agrippina could not think of a response to this that was not sardonic in nature and, knowing how Abigail took everything so personally, decided it was better not to say anything at all. Though Abigail couldn't get her mistress to look upon the prospects of Mr. Maddox as a suitor, she was able to convince her to finally wear the lovely dress her Uncle Rosser, the younger half-brother to Dr. Greystone, gifted her for her birthday earlier that year.

Abigail was convinced the gathering would be a fine

evening, and, therefore, called for a fine dress. Agrippina chose to humor her and allowed the older woman, along with another maid, to do her hair and help her dress with little complaint. When they were done, Agrippina hardly recognized herself. The dress, of the finest muslin, was a dark blue with lace trimmings and—what she thought—unnecessary floral ornaments, but it brought out a pleasing stormy color to her eyes. Her hair, which she often left half wild in Abigail's opinion, was properly pinned and inter-twined with a string of pearls.

If Agrippina had been vainer, she would have fancied herself an image of perfection. But she was not, and sighed against the unknown figure in the mirror.

"There, miss!" Abigail said, pleased with herself. "How handsome you look!"

For her maid's sake, she smiled and thanked her. When she noticed the time, however, she balked.

"Abigail, I am late! Mr. Maddox is sure to have been here for at least a quarter of an hour already."

"Oh, he shall not mind half so much, if at all, once he sees you, miss!"

The other maid smiled and nodded in agreement.

Agrippina sighed and made her way out of her dressing room.

"Oh, miss, do not forget your gloves and fan!" Abigail called after her.

Agrippina stopped and took the purposefully-forgotten items, though a little begrudgingly, and thanked her maid again. She had been right, she found, when she made her way to the drawing room. Mr. Maddox had indeed arrived and had been waiting for her with her uncle. Both of the men stood and gaped at her as she entered.

"Agrippina, you are a vision," her uncle whispered in

astonishment.

"Yes, I feel like a peacock," she replied. She flashed a quick smile at Mr. Maddox. "Shall we go?"

Mr. Maddox nodded. "Yes, directly." He shook Dr. Greystone's hand and ushered Agrippina out where his carriage was waiting for them and handed her into it.

"Wait!" Abigail exclaimed, rushing toward them.

Agrippina held in a groan.

"You must wait for Mr. Bard. He is to act as chaperone." Abigail nodded at them, her brow furrowed in determination.

Agrippina cleared her throat and forced an uncomfortable smile. "I thank you for your consideration, but as a woman who is of age—"

"An unmarried woman."

Agrippina's lip twitched. "As a woman of age, and whose uncle did not seem so concerned as to escort me himself, I am sure our doorman has better things to do than to wait around all night for me to leave a party."

Abigail leaned in so she could whisper. "But, miss, consider what others will think if you are riding around in a carriage with a man who is not your husband. What of your reputation?"

At this, Agrippina smiled. "If riding in a carriage alone with Mr. Maddox is enough to ruin my reputation, then you shall have your way in the end, and I shall force him to marry me."

Mr. Maddox raised a brow in her direction.

"Oh, but, miss!"

"Drive on!" Agrippina called to the driver, tapping the side of the carriage with her hand.

The driver cracked the reins and the horses lurched them forward, leaving Abigail in her disapproval.

Agrippina sighed as she sat back in her seat.

"Force me to marry you?" Mr. Maddox repeated, amused.

"Do not let my comment give you any ideas. It was merely said to rouse a response from my maid."

They were silent for a few minutes until Mr. Maddox found his courage to speak again. "Miss Greystone, had I not witnessed you coming from the house of your uncle, I do not believe I would have recognized you."

"Do not read too much into the alterations in my looks," she replied quickly. "I would not have heard the end of it if I had not allowed my maid the opportunity to dress me up."

Mr. Maddox laughed quietly. "Finery becomes you; regardless of what you say."

"As I am sure you wish it became you."

He laughed harder. "Always a kind word."

Agrippina was shown into the large drawing room of the Hills' and looked upon the scene with tranquil complacency. She, on the other hand, was regarded with a lot more interest. Half of the men in the room turned to look at her, and, even though she knew most of them from her uncle's lectures, they barely recognized her.

"Shall we?" Mr. Maddox said coming up next to her, offering her his arm.

She lifted a suspicious brow but complied, looping her arm through his.

"I believe you have the room's attention, Miss Greystone," Mr. Maddox whispered to her.

With cool calmness she looked about her, noticing several men's eyes fixed on her.

"If the only attention I can claim on these men is due to the prettiness of my face and my figure in this dress, then it only proves to me the shallowness of their character."

Mr. Maddox laughed. "Do you seriously give so little credit to good looks in a person?"

She thought for a moment. "I believe, sometimes, they

are necessary at first in order to attract each other's vanity, but if good looks were all someone had to recommend themselves, then their good looks are rather worthless. If a handsome man upon opening his mouth were to say something utterly intelligible and stupid, I would not give him a second thought."

He stifled another laugh. "Miss Greystone, I do believe this is going to be a very amusing evening."

The dance floor was soon opened and numerous couples moved to join the set. With pleasant surprise did Mr. Maddox find Agrippina to be a suitable partner. She was not as elegant as the other women dancing around them, but still moved with ease and grace. He was not the only one who noticed, and she was soon applied to not long after her dance with Mr. Maddox was over.

"Miss Greystone! I would not have known you!" the young man proclaimed looking her over again.

"Mr. Tilney, that does not surprise me," she replied blandly. "You pay so little attention to anything else I cannot imagine what could catch your notice."

Mr. Maddox stifled a laugh.

The young man smirked. "I supposed you mean your uncle's lectures?" He nodded. "I cannot deny my inattentiveness there."

She didn't reply.

Mr. Tilney cleared his throat. "Might I ask you for the next dance, Miss Greystone? Maddox does not expect you to dance with him the whole night, does he?"

"I do not know why he should if I do not." She glanced at him as more of a challenge than to ask permission.

Mr. Maddox held his hand out. "By all means."

"All right then," she said turning to Mr. Tilney. "We shall see how much attention you can actually pay to something."

Agrippina, though she would never admit it out loud, was enjoying herself. It had been years since she had been to a gathering where she was not the youngest in attendance by at least a decade; her uncle was always bringing her to dinners with his colleagues. Unused to the attentions of young men closer to her age, she was beginning to be flattered, though not taken in.

After her fourth partner, and refusing a fifth, she moved to another room in search of another mode of entertainment. She found it in the billiard room where Mr. Maddox had scampered off.

"Miss Greystone!" he called out when she entered, a pool stick in his hand.

The other men in the room turned.

"I believe the tea room is just down the hall," said one of the young men unknown to her. "That is where the women gather."

"Yes, I passed it on my way here," she replied blandly.

"Oh, let her be, Craft!" cried Mr. Maddox. He waved her over. "Do you know how to play?"

She looked at the table and back at him. Realizing he wanted nothing more than to teach her, she replied she did not.

The other two men groaned while he looked delighted.

"It is not so difficult," he explained. "You shall learn in no time."

After ten minutes of the men going around and teaching her the rules and showing her how to hit, it was proposed they should play a game.

"Miss Greystone, you can be on my team, while Craft and Martin can be on the other," Mr. Maddox suggested.

"Shall we place a bet?" Martin asked.

"Yes! We shall!" said Craft. "Three shillings a person?"

"What? Bet?" Maddox balked. "You will have the lady play for money on her first game?"

"I accept," Agrippina replied without hesitation. "Three shillings is nothing to me, win or lose."

Maddox looked at her in surprise while the other men smirked. Underestimating her was their mistake, however, and after Craft broke, she hit without waiting for Mr. Maddox to finish his instruction on where and how to strike.

The first ball went in.

"We are solids, then?" she asked moving to set up for her next hit without waiting for a reply.

"Beginner's luck," grumbled the one Maddox had been calling Craft.

"I do not believe in luck." She hit and sunk another ball.

Ten minutes later, Agrippina was holding out her hand to receive her winnings from her two astonished adversaries. Even Mr. Maddox looked at her with amazement.

Mr. Craft shook his head. "I cannot believe it. You must have cheated."

Agrippina thought the accusation too stupid to be offended and merely blinked at him. "I am not sure how I could have."

"We play again!" Mr. Martin exclaimed. "Same price."

Agrippina glanced at Mr. Maddox who shrugged. "If you wish to lose again, I am sure there is no harm in playing another round."

After the second round, the billiard room had gathered quite a crowd trying to observe the game. And, after the third, Mr. Craft and Mr. Martin were replaced by two others who soon lost. After the fifth, no one dared to challenge them.

"You are a marvel, Miss Greystone," Mr. Tilney told her after watching her last few plays.

She shrugged. "Billiards is nothing really. It is understanding the angles at which you must hit the ball and the force it will take to get it to where you need it to go. It is simple geometric equations mixed with physics."

Mr. Maddox laughed at her. "That might be the most modest thing I have ever heard you say."

Just then a servant walked into the room with a letter asking if Mr. Maddox was in attendance.

"Here, my good man," he said taking the letter from him. He frowned down at it.

"Who would be writing you a letter at this hour?" Mr. Tilney asked him.

"My sister," Mr. Maddox replied a little gravely. "This is an express from Essex." He hesitated opening it.

"Perhaps, you should like some privacy," Agrippina suggested.

He shook his head as he opened the letter and immediately turned white upon reading its contents.

"Maddox? Has something happened?" Mr. Tilney ventured after Maddox had yet to recover.

Mr. Maddox swallowed. "I must go," he said, suddenly folding the letter up and putting it into his jacket pocket. "I must return to Essex."

Mr. Tilney gawked. "What? Now? It is nearly two in the morning!"

"I cannot delay my journey. Miss Greystone, forgive me, but I must leave at once."

She nodded. "Then we shall go."

"I am sorry to make your evening end sooner than it would have."

"It is nothing," she replied. "I was growing tired anyway. You saved me the trouble of having to ask you to return me home."

With that, the two of them said their goodbyes as Mr. Maddox's carriage was ordered.

"You do not ask me what my letter contained," Mr. Maddox stated as they were on their way.

"Should I?" she replied. "It is none of my business if you do not wish to make it so."

He smiled appreciatively. "You are an oddity, Miss Greystone."

"Hm."

"Might I ask where you learned to play billiards?"

At this she smirked. "I allow you to have your secrets, therefore, you should allow me to have mine."

3

"AGRIPPINA, DEAREST," HER UNCLE SAID AS SHE ENTERED THE breakfast room the next morning. "I hope you had a pleasant evening."

She nodded as she sat. "I won fifteen shillings at billiards."

"Did you?" Her uncle chuckled. "I suppose you did not tell them that you have been playing since you were ten?"

"Of course not. I much prefer the element of stupefaction."

Dr. Greystone laughed harder. "Was bamboozling poor young men out of their pocket money the only enjoyment you had or did you at least dance?"

"There was no bamboozling, uncle," she lightly corrected. "They underestimated my abilities and paid for it dearly. However cheated they might feel is on them."

"Ah."

"And, yes, I danced with a few gentlemen. Some of whom I know from your lessons and one man whose name I have long forgotten and is not worth much more notice than he was an agreeable enough partner."

He shook his head. "You are a harsh judge of character, my dear."

She nodded in agreement. "Yes, well, I suppose if I am to have a flaw, that must be it."

Dr. Greystone tried to suppress a smile but failed. "Yes, and I suppose even an old acquaintance is not even safe from you, are they?"

"How do you mean."

He produced a letter from his jacket pocket. "You must read this and tell me yourself. I am not sure what to think of it." There was a strange smile on her uncle's face as he held out the letter for her. "It came express not long after you left last night."

She hesitated a moment as she put her utensils down and took it from him. "That is rather strange. Mr. Maddox was called away by a letter posted by express as well." She unfolded it and began to read. After half a minute, she looked up at her uncle, a bemused frown on her face.

"Is this a joke, uncle?" she asked.

He shook his head. "I am not sure. Please, read it aloud, for I hardly know what to make of it." He chuckled softly. "I believe I read it several times last night wishing you were home to enjoy it with me."

Agrippina cleared her throat.

"Dr. Greystone,

I understand it has been a few years since our last correspondence, but something of the most peculiar circumstance has come up, and, without hesitation, I thought of you. It has come to the crown's attention that the town of Blindburn, on the very most northern border of England and Scotland, has been plagued with the similarly strange deaths of no more than five young women.

"The town, as small and ignorant of the world as they may be, is convinced they have a werewolf."

"Oh, uncle, honestly!" Agrippina almost laughed looking

up from the letter. "A werewolf? Can you imagine?"

Dr. Greystone pressed his lips together to keep from laughing. "Do not yet judge what you do not understand, Agrippina, my dear," he playfully scolded her. "Continue."

"Five young women have all been found with what has been described as deep slash wounds to their faces, and torso. The slash wounds appear to be from some kind of animal like that of a wolf though are said to be larger like that of an unnatural creature.

"As you are a man of sound mind and steady observation, I immediately volunteered your name to the king's consort as he is a close family friend and asked my father for his advice on whom to send. I often think fondly back to your stories of investigating strange circumstances with your brother so there is no doubt in my mind of your capabilities.

"This, of course, will be a paid assignment. If I have piqued your interest, you can write to the address attached to this note, or if it is not too much of an inconvenience, I shall be in Cambridge a day or two after you have received this letter. I would very much like to see you again, and Miss Greystone, if she is still at home. We can then go from there.

Your friend,

Thomas Beresford"

"Dear Lord!" Agrippina exclaimed putting the letter down. "Little Lord Thomas Beresford still believing in silly stories."

Dr. Greystone chuckled. "I do not believe he is so little as you remember," he pointed out. "You have not seen him for almost seven years. When I saw him only three years ago, he was half a foot taller than me."

"Well, you are not so tall yourself, uncle," she mused.

He smirked at her.

"And are you to take the assignment?" she asked after a moment, finally preparing her breakfast plate.

He thought for a moment. "An investigation into a possible werewolf? It seems rather interesting to me. What do you think, my dear?"

Agrippina rubbed her lips together for a moment. "It would certainly be a change from grading the papers of over-privileged, little lords for drunken professors," she replied hesitantly, not wanting to give into the excitement she was feeling.

Her uncle nodded. "Agreed."

"And it would be in the interest of the crown if we did."

Her uncle grinned. "For King and country then?" he said holding up his teacup.

Agrippina mimicked her uncle's gesture. "For king and country."

4

True to his word, Lord Thomas Beresford arrived at Dr. Greystone's house the next day. The young man was a far cry from the scrappy boy of seventeen that she had remembered, but the smile was very much the same.

He entered the parlor and greeted them with great fervor, shaking Dr. Greystone's hand enthusiastically. "It is very nice to see you again, sir," he said. "And you, Miss Greystone," he blushed slightly. "I have heard great things about your beauty and I am rather surprised they have been half as correct. Though I have always thought you—well, you have truly blossomed."

Agrippina nodded, smiling with the pleasure of seeing an old friend.. "It is nice to see you again, too, Thomas. Though I am not sure of whom we both know that would be telling you of my beauty. Seems a rather boring thing to talk about."

Lord Beresford, Thomas, laughed. "I am also glad to see your humor has not changed." He took a seat. "I must confess that I come to Cambridge at least once a year on business and I have asked about you on more than one occasion." Again, he blushed.

Her uncle looked from his niece to their visitor.

"Have you?" Agrippina asked a little surprised.

"You seem to be well known around here," he continued.

"If you say you visit so often, why is it you have never come and visited my uncle and me?" she inquired with a raised brow. "We were always good friends you and I." She gave a small pout.

He smiled, though looked a little ashamed. "To be honest, I tried calling on more than one occasion, but, as my luck would have it, you were never at home and I failed to leave a card both times."

"Well, shame on you, Thomas!" she gently scolded. "I suppose all of those years learning and playing together meant nothing."

He smiled, sensing she was not being as harsh as she was portraying. "You spent most of those years teasing me."

She frowned slightly. "Did I?"

He nodded. "Yes, and I believe the last time we met, as you were leaving my father's estate, you told me I was a silly boy who will one day grow to be a silly man and marry a silly woman and have silly children."

"No!" She shook her head. "I cannot believe I said something like that! Uncle, please help me out with this. That does not sound like me!"

Her uncle smirked. "Those may not have been your exact words, my dear, but I was witness to them."

"Aha!" Lord Beresford clasped his hands together. "You see? You were a very teasing girl." He wagged a finger at her.

Agrippina gave a subtle smile. "Well, I would not have said it if I did not believe it to be true."

He grinned.

"And was I right?" she asked. "Are you a silly man with a silly wife?"

His grin turned into a full-fledged smile. "No, just a silly man. I have yet to find my silly wife."

Agrippina laughed through her nose.

Though he was enjoying the ridiculous flirtations of his niece and their prestigious guest, Dr. Greystone was ready to get down to business and cleared his throat to gain the others' attentions. "We have decided, Lord Beresford, to accept your assignment."

The young man looked over at his former teacher with delight. "Have you?" he asked, frowning after what he had said sunk in. "Both of you then?" He smiled. "I should have known the bright, independent Miss Greystone would never refuse a moment to prove someone wrong."

Agrippina raised her brow. "That is a rather harsh view of me you have, Thomas," she replied. "How terrible you must think me. Teasing, arrogant Agrippina Greystone. I wonder why you would ask about me to anyone ever."

"You misunderstand me," he laughed. "I have always admired your tenacity."

"Now I know you are lying," she called him out. "You were always rather cross with me because I was always getting better marks than you."

"I cannot deny I was envious," he agreed, "but it was only because you took to lessons quicker than I could. I had to spend hours studying, yet, you absorbed everything you heard or read."

"Thank you, Thomas," she replied. "That is something I would much rather hear than how pretty I am."

"Absolutely, I have no doubt you would be a great help to your uncle on this investigation."

"Do you have any more information for us other than what you wrote in your letter?" Dr. Greystone asked.

He shook his head. "I am afraid not. I wished to take

the letter my father's friend Lord Helston received, but he would not part with it," he explained. "It was written by one of the noble landowners, I believe. Though I cannot recall his name. It had a Scottish ring to it."

Agrippina lifted a brow and curled her lips into a half smirk. "You do not believe this town to have a werewolf, do you?" she goaded. "You do not still believe in such silly things?"

Lord Beresford smiled and bowed his head. "There is so much of the world I have yet to see, Miss Greystone. I try not to discount anything. But the fact the attacks all happened on a full moon is rather curious."

"All of them on a full moon?" Dr. Greystone asked. "You did not mention that in your letter."

Lord Beresford frowned. "Did I not?" He shook his head. "Forgive me. I thought I would have. It is important information, to be sure."

"A mere coincidence," Agrippina concluded. "Full moons are not rare, you know."

Dr. Greystone gave an absent-minded nod.

"When do you leave?" Lord Beresford asked. "I can write to Lord Helston and have him send the letter to you, or at least have it copied and sent."

"There is no need! I wrote to him of our acceptance soon after I received your letter. Besides, we leave early tomorrow morning," he answered, amused with the young lord's reaction. "I suppose it will take us about a fortnight to get there."

"Tomorrow?" he repeated, slightly surprised. "You are leaving so soon?"

"Is there something wrong?" Dr. Greystone replied.

Lord Beresford gave a slight shake of the head. "No, it is just that I was thinking I might come along. However, my business here would not be concluded for another few days."

"As this matter is of urgency," Agrippina stepped in, "I think it best we do not delay our journey. Perhaps, you could meet us up there after your business is over."

Beresford nodded. "I suppose I could." He smiled. "If not, you must write to me of your progress. And when you are finished, perhaps you could come to London. I am sure my father would be delighted to see you both again. He does often reminisce about the time you spent with us."

"Not with fondness, I imagine," Agrippina said with a nod. "Your father often seemed provoked by me."

Lord Beresford laughed. "That is because you often provoked him!" He shook his head. "I am true to my word, however. My father thought you an amusing child and often wonders if you turned into an amusing young woman."

"I have heard the term eccentric, or strange, uttered in my presence when I have been thought to be out of earshot," she replied. "I cannot say that I have heard the term amusing and my name in the same sentence."

"My niece it too modest," Dr. Greystone interceded. "I often talk about how amusing she is with other professors. Amongst our circle, she is one of the most amusing persons of our acquaintance."

"Uncle, I hardly think your opinion counts," Agrippina said. "You have raised me as your own since I was seven. You have a father's affections toward me which makes you view everything about me in a positive light. You are too biased to make an accurate judgement."

Her uncle frowned pensively. "My opinion does not count?" he repeated, feigning offense. "That is rather hurtful to a man who thinks too much of his opinion to be told otherwise."

Lord Beresford laughed. "I think your opinion counts

more than anyone else's!" he proclaimed. "If your uncle deems you as amusing, then I shall believe him and consider you so as well."

Dr. Greystone smiled.

The young man rose. "Now, if you will forgive me, I must be going."

"Are you already leaving?" Dr. Greystone asked, disappointed he could not stay. "You only just arrived."

"Unfortunately, I must," Lord Beresford replied. "I have a prior engagement, or else I might invite myself to dinner." He smiled. "It has truly been a pleasure to see you both again." He bowed. "I look forward to your letters."

"Good day to you, Thomas," Agrippina replied with a small curtsey.

Dr. Greystone watched him go with great interest, while his niece picked up the book she had been reading before Lord Beresford's entrance and continued where she left off.

"I think I much like Lord Beresford, Aggy," Dr. Greystone said the next morning as they prattled along in the carriage. "He has grown into a pleasant young man. Good humored with just the right amount of seriousness about him."

"Yes, it appears he has outgrown his awkward stage," she replied, watching the scenes of Cambridge slipping away in the distance. "Though that does not make him any less silly."

"I beg to differ. He seems to have taken a liking to you which is another thing to like him for. It tells me he is a sensible man," he pointed out. "And I do believe you were flirting back with him."

Agrippina turned her gaze to her uncle. "Uncle, I do not flirt," she told him bluntly.

"I might be getting old, but I daresay I know what flirting is when I see it."

She sighed, but refused to reply.

"Is he to be your new beau, then?" he asked her with a raised brow, ignoring her narrowed gaze.

"Uncle!" Agrippina scolded.

"I must say you have had more handsome ones," her uncle continued. "Though he will make you a gallant beau. And he comes with a very nice title. A duke. How prestigious. Your new beau the duke."

"Do not call them 'beaus,'" she pleaded sternly. "I detest the word."

"What shall I call them then?" he pondered. "Suitors?"

Agrippina gave her uncle a blank stare. "Absolutely not. That would imply my intentions were serious."

"Flirtations then?"

"No, please, stop," she urged. "You are now making me out to be some silly girl floating from one whim to the next."

"Then what would you call them, my dear?" her uncle pressed, amused and unwilling to let the subject drop.

Aggy huffed out of loving annoyance for her uncle. "If I had to call them anything, which I would much rather not, I would call them pleasant male acquaintances in whose company I might have blushed for more than a moment in their presence."

Her uncle laughed. "Well, that hardly rolls off the tongue, does it?" he replied. "No, I will never be able to remember all of that. I shall call them 'relishers.'"

"Relishers, uncle?" Agrippina made a face, displeased with her uncle's teasing.

"Yes, for I would never call them lovers; that is too serious for you."

She lifted a brow at him.

"Relishers will have to do, for they briefly relished in the light of your beautiful, yet, rare smile."

"This is going to be a very long fortnight," Agrippina muttered.

Dr. Greystone chuckled. "There is nothing wrong with letting your defenses down, my dear, and falling in love. It has happened more than once over the history of mankind and we are still in existence. Love has never harmed anyone."

Agrippina lifted her brows. "I believe the Trojans would beg to differ."

5

Dr. Greystone and his niece made it to Blindburn a little more than a fortnight later due to some bad weather along the way. Despite the rainy weather, however, the ride was pleasant and the roads were tolerable which made for an uneventful journey.

Once they arrived, they were shown to a local inn where they inquired after a couple of rooms. The innkeeper, a rotund widow no older than forty-five, seemed a little confused by her guests as she had never expected company with the reports of what was happening around town. She did not hesitate, though, to show them her two finest rooms.

"I 'ope these will do fer ya, sir," she said as she opened the doors and allowed them to peer in.

"They are very well, ma'am," Dr. Greystone replied with a polite nod of his head. "We are much obliged to you."

"I can 'ave refreshments brought up in a few minutes if you'd like," the woman, who had introduced herself as Winifred Bragg, said. "I imagine you 'ad a long journey from wherever 'tis you come from."

"We traveled all the way from Cambridge, ma'am," he

explained. "We have been hired, you see, to investigate the mysterious deaths of those young women."

Mrs. Bragg blanched for a moment before turning red. "Blessed be," she whispered. "Can our prayers be answered?" Tears welled in her eyes. "'Tis an awful thing these killin's, sir. My own cousin's daughter, God rest 'er poor soul, was one o' the victims."

"Is that so?" Dr. Greystone inquired.

"Aye, sir." She bowed her head. "She were the second I b'lieve. Terrible business. My cousin didn' knocw what ta do wi' 'erself. She's still lost in 'er 'eart, sir. Terrible business."

Dr. Greystone nodded. "Do you know where I might start my inquiries?" he asked. "I am afraid I do not know much about the case other than the mode of death."

She nodded. "I would go to the vicar, sir," she told him. "'e knows much 'bout the killin's."

"Very good, Mrs. Bragg," Dr. Greystone praised. "We shall go there directly, once we freshen up."

Mrs. Bragg blinked for a moment before she turned her attention to Agrippina who was just coming back out of her room from depositing her things. She thought it strange that a young woman was going to be joining on such unpleasant business. She even wondered if she had missed a third person in their party, but knew she had not.

She did not, however, question them. It was not her place to question those of a higher class than herself. Besides, they were paying customers and she could not afford to offend them.

Once they were done freshening up, Dr. Greystone and Agrippina made their way to the vicar, ready with directions from the innkeeper. They were both silent for a moment as they walked, looking around them at the small town with scattered little houses and rolling hills.

"It is certainly beautiful here," Dr. Greystone stated.

"Yes, though it is very far from Cambridge, and, I have to say, very far from its society," Agrippina commented.

Her uncle laughed. "We have only met with one person and you already judge them harshly. Come now, my girl, open your mind a bit. Not everyone can afford a Lord's education, but that does not mean they should be open to ridicule."

"This is what you say about people who believe they have a werewolf in their midst?" She lifted a critical brow at her uncle.

"Come, come! Try to have a little imagination." He laughed until he broke into a fit of coughing and he had to stop to catch his breath. "Forgive me."

"Uncle, you have done that more than once on our ride up here," she pointed out. "And you look unusually pale."

He nodded. "I am all right." He cleared his throat. "I am just not used to the clean air up here yet."

"Are you sure?" she pressed, trying not to sound too concerned. "We can come back tomorrow after you have rested."

He squeezed her shoulder. "I shall live. Besides, time is of the essence. We must talk to those connected to the case while it is still fresh in their minds. Or, as fresh as they can be really."

Agrippina, though uneasy, was forced to concede to her uncle and let the subject drop.

After half a mile's walk, they came to a small chapel on the hill overlooking the river Croquet. It was the quaint-est sight Agrippina could ever remember seeing. Despite its Godly aesthetic, made more beautiful by the natural scene in which it was placed, Agrippina knew God was not going to meet them within the walls of that church.

She felt it even more so as a cold wind blew from on top of the hill, causing her to shiver. The wind, she felt, was a more accurate representation of the kind of greeting they would find when they entered the little building's stone walls.

They were met just before the entrance by a tall, thin man with wispy white hair and a scowl for a face. "Might I help you folks?" he asked skeptically.

"Good day to you, sir," Dr. Greystone said in reply. "My name is Doctor Alfred Greystone and this my niece Agrippina Greystone. We have hailed all the way from Cambridge to help you and your parishioners sort out the troubles you are having."

The vicar's scowl deepened. "What troubles could you be alluding to, sir?"

"The dead women, sir."

"I do not know why the poor young souls of those unknown to you would concern you at all. Why, I would never travel to Cambridge to stick my nose into one of your deaths."

Agrippina let out a small sigh, causing the sharp eye of the vicar to fall on her. She had been right.

"Be that as it may, vicar—I am sorry, I do not know your name," Dr. Greystone pointed out.

"Vicar Harmon will do."

Dr. Greystone nodded. "Yes, be that as it may, Vicar Harmon, we have been sent by the crown to investigate and I am afraid we cannot leave until we have done so, and done so thoroughly."

"Humph, I see," the vicar replied haughtily. "Well, I could have saved you the trouble had you taken the time to write first, but I guess you southerners think you are too good for all of that."

"I am sorry, save us the trouble, did you say?" Dr.

Greystone repeated.

"Yes, there is no need for your investigation," the vicar arrogantly told them. "We have already caught our culprit."

"You seem rather proud, sir," Agrippina pointed out. "Is pride not a sin?"

Anger flashed through the vicar's eyes. "There can be no sin in priding over God's work!" he proclaimed.

"Very well, if you please," Dr. Greystone said, shooting his niece a quieting look. "But, pray, tell us who this culprit is."

"An old vagabond woman, a witch," he triumphed.

"A witch?" Agrippina repeated, trying not to laugh as she did.

"Aye," the vicar shot another look at her. "A witch, a woman who lies with the devil and does his bidding."

"And you believe this witch controls the werewolf that has been terrorizing the town?" Agrippina pressed.

"Of course! She confessed it all!" He glared at her. "She has confessed to transforming into this beast on the full moon and murdering these poor girls to satiate her bloodlust."

Agrippina shook her head in slight confusion. "Well, what is she? Is she a witch or is she a werewolf? Surely, she cannot be both?"

The vicar's nostrils flared. "With the power of the devil guiding her? Certainly she can be both. And as I have already stated, she has confessed."

"Yes, you mentioned that, but was that before or after you tortured her?" Aggy questioned coldly.

The vicar glared at her.

"Yes, I know how these interrogations go," she told him. "She says no, so you singe her with a hot poker, or break the bones in her hands, or whip her until she speaks."

The glare from the vicar only became stronger.

"So which mode of 'interrogation' did you employ?"

"I will not bear a catechism coming from a woman. I told you how it is and what was said. The woman confessed." Vicar Harmon turned his head, and refused to look at her again.

"Under torture, I dare say she did confess," Aggy stated, indifferent to his cold manner toward her. "And if I were to torture you, you would damn near say anything to get me to stop, but more particularly what I wanted to hear."

The vicar looked horrified by Agrippina's mode of speech. "Not only that!" he proclaimed. "She has the mark of the devil! A red mark just above her navel. I have seen it myself!"

"A birthmark, no doubt," Agrippina retorted without delay. "She has probably had it since she was born and there is nothing she can do about that. A natural defect, nothing to do with the devil whatsoever. Any educated man could have known that."

The vicar opened his mouth to fire back when he was interrupted by Dr. Greystone.

"Well, then," he began, clearing his throat and stopping his niece from further damaging their relationship with the locals, "shall we see this woman? Where are you harboring her?"

The vicar looked hesitant to comply.

"Allow me to remind you, Vicar Harmon, that we are here on the crown's orders and any interference could be punished severely."

The vicar twitched for a moment but relented. "She's out back in the storage shed."

"What? She's here?" Agrippina asked, giving her uncle an alarmed look.

"Might you be so kind as to show us to her?" Dr. Greystone inquired graciously, more than the vicar deserved.

Grumbling, Vicar Harmon acquiesced and took them to a

small wooden shack in the back of the church property, just before the graveyard that stretched over the hill. The shack looked half dilapidated; its roof was most likely leaking and there were enough holes in the walls to render them useless. This small shed, meant for storage of minor tools and unfit for a dog, was where the poor woman unlucky enough to be without protection had been chained to.

The vicar opened the door and let in the gray light from the cloudy sky shine in the sad room. The stench that wafted from its confinement washed over the three of them, and Agrippina had to cover her nose with her handkerchief to keep from gagging.

There was a clinking sound as the chained woman moved inside her prison and into the light; it fell upon her bruised, dirty face. She flinched at first, her eyes only adjusted to the darkness of her shack.

"You see there?" the vicar pointed out. "You see how she shies away from the light? She is a witch." He spat on the ground next to him.

"No, no! Not I!" the woman moaned pitifully. "Not I, please!"

"Shut up, witch!" Vicar Harmon hissed. "Or I shall beat you again!"

"Perhaps, vicar, you would let us talk to the poor wretch alone," Dr. Greystone suggested. "I do not want our interviewee to be pressured by an outside party."

The vicar blinked at him for a moment. "Fine. But don't blame me if this woman casts a spell on you. Though I would be worrying more about the young lady. Women, as weak as their minds are, are more susceptible to the powers of evil."

Agrippina glared at him, her handkerchief still pressed against her face. "Uncle," she whispered harshly when the vicar walked away, "this poor woman."

Her uncle nodded and stepped closer. "Good afternoon, ma'am," he began, struggling not to cough at the smell of human filth. "I have come to ask you a few questions if you do not mind."

The woman nodded weakly. "Might I 'ave some water first, sir?" she replied in a shaky voice, crumpled on the dirt floor of the shack.

Agrippina looked around and found a well where she quickly retrieved a bucket of water and ladled a few mouthfuls into the poor woman's mouth.

"Bless ye, deary," she told her, trying not to cry by her kindness.

"What is your name, madam, so that I might properly address you?" Dr. Greystone asked.

"Me mother called me Bertie, sir," she replied meekly. "Bertie will do, if you please."

"I do please, Bertie," Dr. Greystone responded. "I am sorry we must meet in such awful circumstances."

The woman began to cry. "They've done awful things to me, sir!" she exclaimed without provocation. "Though I know nothin' of the evil things they 'cuse me of!"

"It is all right, Bertie," Dr. Greystone reassured her gently. "I am here with my niece to investigate the murders of which you have been accused."

"Oh, bless ye, sir, and, miss! Bless ye both!"

Dr. Greystone nodded. "How long have you lived here in Blindburn, Bertie?" he asked as Agrippina gently ladled more water into the woman's mouth.

"I come 'ere a couple times uh year, sir," she replied. "'Twas born in Scotland, but I 'ave a beggar's license," she explained.

"And when did you come back to Blindburn this time?" he continued his query.

"After Lughnasadh, but before Samhain, sir. I be sure of i'."

"Lughnasadh?" Agrippina repeated, finally speaking. "That starts August first. The first of the killings happened in November a year ago and then every three months since, did they not?"

Her uncle nodded. "You said you come here every year, Bertie?"

The woman nodded. "Aye, sir. Though the folk used to be kinder."

"Do you know why they accuse you?" Agrippina asked.

The woman shook her head. "No, miss!" she wailed. "I be uh good person!"

"Well, Bertie, we are going to try and help you best we can," Dr. Greystone told her.

"Please, sir," she moaned, reaching out her mangled, broken hand to Dr. Greystone. "I've not done it. They 'cuse me of awful things I've not done."

Dr. Greystone gently held the woman's battered hand in his own. "We believe you, my dear," he told her with calm feeling. "We will not let you rot here."

"Oh, bless ye, sir!" the poor old woman cried. "God bless ye!"

Agrippina left the bucket of water and ladle for the woman to drink from freely, and followed her uncle back to the church. "These people are barbaric!" she exclaimed. "Did you see the condition that poor woman was in?"

Her uncle nodded. "Yes, and then left outside in this weather, tethered like a dog." He gave an exasperated sigh. "We certainly are very far from Cambridge."

They entered the church and found the vicar straightening up the pulpit. Agrippina's stomach churned at the sight. She could not imagine someone as him being allowed to preach the word of God knowing what monstrosities he had allowed just behind his precious little church. She shivered as she saw the vicar basking in the red glow of the stained-glass windows.

"And what did we learn?" the vicar asked, not looking up from what he was doing.

"We learned that Bertie did not arrive in Blindburn until *after* the killings began," Agrippina said before her uncle could. "Several months, in fact. How she could have killed those women when she was not even in town must be-"

"An act of the Devil?" the vicar finished for her. "Yes, I am aware she was not in town, but do not underestimate the power of evil and its destructive forces. You do not have to be in a specific town to wreak havoc upon it with the blessings of the Lord of Darkness."

Agrippina scoffed lightly. "If I am to be honest, vicar, your accent and mode of speech sounds intelligent, but the words you speak are not. Your antiquated mode of thinking and belief in the supernatural assures me that you are a supercilious fool who is no more educated than a child who believes in fairytales."

The vicar looked taken aback a moment before anger washed over his face. "I will not be talked to like that by a woman."

Dr. Greystone cleared his throat in warning to his niece not to respond. "What is to happen to Bertie, vicar?" he asked trying to keep the conversation on track.

"She will be tried, of course, as a witch," he replied matter-of-factly.

"You cannot hang her as a witch," Agrippina claimed. "The prosecution of those believed to be practicing in magic was outlawed in the 1730's with the Witchcraft Act which, in turn, makes it punishable to accuse someone of being a witch."

Vicar Harmon turned red. "Being a witch might not be illegal by mortal standards anymore, but it is by God's. Regardless, she will be tried for *murder*, tried and, when found guilty, hanged."

"Do you mean she will be hanged *if* she is found guilty?" Agrippina corrected.

The vicar sucked his teeth. "If, yes."

"And when is this 'trial' to be?" Agrippina asked coldly.

"In two days."

Agrippina and her uncle exchanged glances.

"Then it must be delayed," Dr. Greystone stated with authority. "We have come to investigate, and we will not have a trial before a proper investigation has been conducted, or I shall write the crown and tell the king that you explicitly disobeyed his orders which could most assuredly result in treason."

At this the vicar paled, his mouth opening and closing in confusion as he stuttered through what to say. "T-t-treason?" he finally choked out. "I have never in my life thought of taking such action!"

"Well, then we have an accord," Dr. Greystone said with a nod. "You shall hold off with your trial until we give you further notice. You should also release Miss Bertie into our care. We shall vouch for her innocence."

"You have no authority to-"

"As you did not have permission to make an arrest in this case, you have no authority to hold her," Dr. Greystone concluded. "She will come back with us at once." Dr. Greystone stood straighter; his face set sternly as he stared down the vicar.

After a moment, the vicar conceded, begrudgingly. "Fine, you can have your witch!" he snarled. "But do not come crying to me for a blessing when she curses the both of you!"

"Duly noted, sir," Dr. Greystone retorted indifferently.

There was a tense silence between the three of them.

Agrippina cleared her throat and gave a small nod of her head.

Her uncle took the hint. "Yes, well, it seems I might also be troubling you with a list of the unfortunate women who befell this mysterious beast of yours. Mrs. Bragg told us you were the person to talk to, after all."

The vicar glared at him, unmoving.

"Might I remind you, sir, that if you hinder with our investigation, we will have you arrested and dragged down to London for a trial of your own," Agrippina told him sharply.

The vicar's lip twitched a moment before he bowed his head and walked into a back office. He returned not much longer with a piece of paper; five names scrawled on it.

"Here," he said gruffly. "Now if you do not mind, leave my church immediately."

Dr. Greystone took the paper with a short bow. "I shall send a carriage for Miss Bertie," he said as he and his niece turned and walked out.

"That poor woman, uncle," Agrippina declared as they walked back out into the gray afternoon. "Why, she is already found guilty before a trial. You heard it in his voice, I am sure."

He nodded with a sigh. "I did."

She shook her head. "To call himself a vicar! A man of God! Why it is almost laughable. What power he thinks he has."

He nodded again. "I think we shall call it a day for now," he told her. "This interview has made me rather tired."

Agrippina slipped her arm through her uncle's. "Lean on me," she told him. "I am too angry to be tired."

6

Bertie was indeed fetched for and brought to the inn, and, at first, Mrs. Bragg refused her entrance, but a quick word about another room being rented out gave way to her superstitions as times were hard and customers were scarce.

She quickly drew the haggard, old woman a bath and disposed of her ragged clothes, giving her an old dress of hers to wear instead. Mrs. Bragg then served them all warm supper and tea.

Bertie found it difficult to eat with most of her teeth having already rotted out, and her broken hand making it difficult to cut, but she graciously cried through the whole ordeal.

"I've ne'er met wi' such kindness," she sobbed as she spooned a piece of bread that had been soaking in broth into her mouth. "Not since me own mother!"

"There, there, Miss Bertie," Dr. Greystone hushed gently.

"God bless ye three," she continued to cry as she ate.

"How do Bertie's wounds look, Uncle Al?" Agrippina asked later that evening as she fluffed her uncle's pillows. "They are not so terribly bad, are they?"

"Huh," he replied, stirring from the chair from which he had been reading. "Oh, right, yes. The poor woman's hand will take a long time to heal. But I believe you did well setting it. And her scrapes are quite superficial."

"I am glad," she replied as she straightened up the desk by the far wall, placing on it her uncle's inks and quills and papers. "Whom shall we visit tomorrow first?"

"I spoke to Mrs. Bragg, and she seems to think that the father of Missy Hodgkin—Percy, I believe she said—would be a good place to start. She said he has the strongest voice of them all since this began. Even before his daughter met with her unfortunate fate. I have already sent a note requesting he meet us here tomorrow morning at nine."

"Good!" Agrippina said cheerfully.

Her uncle noticed the inflection and turned to her from where he sat. "This amuses you, does it not?"

Agrippina avoided his gaze, turning her attention to the darkness coming in through the window. "I must admit, I have never thought of doing something like this," she replied. "I have traveled, you know. You have sent me all over the continent and I have lived my life among some of the most brilliant minds. I have visited ancient cities and studied ruins, but this- this is different. It- well, it," she paused, "it makes me feel closer to papa." She gave him a somber look. "I know that seems silly, him being dead for so long, but I remember the stories you used to tell me. About the strange adventures the two of you would go on. The mysteries you would solve."

Her uncle smiled lovingly at her. "That is not silly, my dear," he told her affectionately. "Far from it." He grunted a bit as he stood from the chair. "In fact, it makes me happy to hear you say it. You rarely ever talk about your father nowadays." He took her hand and patted it. "He would be very proud of you."

"I am not ashamed to say I know that," she replied, a small, close-lipped smile on her face, "but it is still nice to hear it regardless."

Dr. Greystone chuckled.

"Did you ever encounter an investigation like this before?" she asked.

Dr. Greystone thought for a moment. "We investigated a few murders or mysterious deaths, but nothing compared to a possible werewolf," he replied with a grin.

Agrippina sighed. "What do you think he would have said about this? Would he have laughed off the superstition as well?"

Dr. Greystone smiled at the floor as he remembered. "No, not at first," he told her. "Your father, as practical as he was- as smart as he was- always kept an open mind. He knew there was enough in this world that we do not understand- that science had yet to prove. He was a logical person, but he did not let that cloud his beliefs."

Agrippina frowned. "What do you mean?"

"Sometimes, the logical explanation is not always the correct one," he explained. "Your father understood that."

She blinked at him for a moment before shaking her head. "I still am not sure what that means."

"Do not let it bother you too much, my dear," her told her as her kissed her forehead. "I think I shall call it a night. We have a long day ahead of us. Several long days to be exact."

She nodded. "Good night, uncle," she said as she left the room, quietly closing the door behind her.

"Excuse me, miss."

Agrippina felt her skin prickle a moment in fear and gasped as she turned to see the innkeeper standing behind her, her face aglow in the candle she was holding.

"Forgive me. I didn' mean tuh startle ya," she began a little uneasily. "But I found these hanging from yours and your uncle's doorknobs." She held up two stones with holes in them dangling from a piece of string. "I belie'e that woman done it."

Agrippina took the stones in her hand. They were not large, but they were smooth to the touch, and the holes appeared to be made naturally. They must have been river rocks.

She looked back up at the innkeeper. "These are harmless, Mrs. Bragg," she reassured her. "If I am being honest, Bertie put them there out of consideration for my uncle and myself. They are old Scottish talismans for protection. Though these are more likely to be seen on the door of a barn, I do believe she meant to help us." She pondered for a moment where Bertie could have retrieved the stones. Surely they weren't on her person this whole time.

The innkeeper looked uncomfortable.

"Think nothing of it, Mrs. Bragg," Agrippina told her, putting one of the stones back on her uncle's knob. "I am rather touched Bertie thought so much of us to give us such a rare stone."

"But what're those things s'pose to protect you from?" the innkeeper asked.

At this Agrippina chuckled softly. "From witches."

7

Percy Hodgkin did not disappoint and arrived promptly at the inn at nine the next morning. He wiped his feet and took off his ragged hat as he entered, revealing his shaggy auburn hair. His clothes appeared worn but clean, and he stood tall and proud.

"Mornin' to ya, sir, miss," he said in greeting, nodding subtly as he was shown to the Greystones.

Dr. Greystone bowed as Agrippina gave a small curtsey.

"It is a pleasure to meet you, Mr. Hodgkin," Dr. Greystone said. "Though I wish the meeting was under better circumstances."

"Thank you, sir," Mr. Hodgkin replied, bowing his head. "There are some that be glad yer 'ere. Though others be skeptical, sir, them thinkin' the witch be the cause, it ne'er settled with me. Ol' Ber'ie ne'er hurt no one. I known 'er fer years."

"Might we offer you something to eat or drink, Mr. Hodgkin?" Dr. Greystone graciously asked.

"Very kind 'o you, sir, but I be fine."

Agrippina blinked. "Beg your pardon, but you still referred

53

to Bertie as a witch, did you not?" she pointed out.

"Aye," Hodgkin said with a nod. "She be a white witch, ma'am. She does good magic. People 'ere know tha', but when panic sets in wi' fear, you forget who yer friends are."

Agrippina nodded. "Of course."

"'Tis told you rescued 'er from 'er li'l cell," Hodgkin stated. "Some o' us be right glad you did."

"Word spreads fast here, I see," Dr. Geystone replied. "Yes, Bertie is asleep upstairs."

"Are the others very angry?" Agrippina asked.

"Beg yer pardon, miss?"

"You said some are glad we had Bertie released," she repeated. "Are the others quite angry?"

"Ah, well, thee others might belie'e we don' need outside 'elp and twould 'ave been bet'er if you 'ad stayed wherever you come from." He wrung his worn hat in his hands. "They'll get over i'. They'll see they was wrong 'bout poor ol' Ber'ie."

"Right, then," Dr. Greystone said, clapping his hands together. "Shall we get going, Agrippina? Are you ready?"

"Yes, uncle," she replied with a nod.

Hodgkin frowned. "Beg yer pardon fer askin' but what business does she 'ave goin' out wi' us?"

"The same business you have, I would imagine," Agrippina curtly replied.

Hodgkin looked in alarm at Dr. Greystone.

"Yes, yes," her uncle declared with a wave of his hand trying to rush the explanation along. "My niece has about as much business to come as anyone. She is very intelligent, and nothing surpasses her notice. She must come."

"But she be a woman, sir," Hodgkin all but whispered.

"What acute observation skills you have, Mr. Hodgkin," Agrippina told him sardonically. "I am indeed a woman."

"Woman's place be in the kitchen, in the 'ome, sir, not out

tryin' to solve murders."

Agrippina took in a calming breath, her mouth twitching. "If I was of a lower class, sir, I dare say my place would be in the kitchen. Be that as it may, as a woman of wealth and class, I would hire someone—much like your wife if you have one—to do all of the cooking for me. Therefore, my place will never be in the kitchen." She picked up her bag from the table and started for the door. "Now, unless you wish to stand here all day and determine the color of my hair, I suggest we go."

Doctor Greystone smiled. "My niece has quite the sense of humor, but I assure you, there is no one better for this job in all of Europe." He made a gesture with his hand to Hodgkin as if telling him to lead the way.

Hodgkin looked put out at having to obey the demands of an overbearing woman, but followed obediently, if not begrudgingly.

Fifteen minutes later, Hodgkin banged on the side of carriage to alert the driver to stop.

"'Tis just 'round the corner, over there, sir," he said indicating with his head. "I thought it be best to walk from 'ere."

"Ah, right you are. Thank you, Mr. Hodgkin," Dr. Greystone replied.

The driver opened the door and handed Agrippina out first.

She stood to the side and observed the bend in the road disappearing between two tall, grass-covered hills. "How far is this spot from where your daughter was going, Mr. Hodgkin?" she asked pulling out a small journal and pencil from her bag.

"'ome is not far from 'ere," he replied. "Our house be a fifteen-minute walk in that direction." He pointed. "But, at the time, I belie'e she were goin' to the pub to meet her intended. Which be no more than ten minutes."

He led them further along the road between the hills a hundred yards or so where they left the carriage and stopped, removing his hat and bowing his head.

"This is where it happened?" Dr. Greystone asked looking around the valley with the high hills on both sides.

"Aye, 'tis. 'ere 'bouts somewhere," Hodgkin replied somberly. "Me poor little lass, didn' stand no chance again' what took 'er." His voice trembled as he spoke.

"Who found her?" Agrippina questioned, surveying the scene. The road that ran through the valley curved into it, making it difficult to see around the corner as the hills were too high.

"'Twer 'er sweet'eart come lookin' fer 'er and foun' 'er all covered in blood." At this, Hodgkin began to cry freely. His tears- long held back- flowed easily down his unshaven cheek. "She were a good girl," he croaked. "Never 'urt a soul. Too good for me an' this world. Must be why God saw it fit to take 'er from me." He wiped his face. "I almost couldna belie'e it were 'er when I saw 'er. I thought, that can' be my girl, not mine."

"I imagine it was a great shock to you," Agrippina said, trying to sound sympathetic.

"Aye, but that were not it," he replied. "I couldna recognize 'er." His voice began to shake harder. "She no longer 'ad a face. 'er pretty face were gone." He let out an anguished sob. "'er pretty face were covered in gashes." He cleared his throat and his voice fell to a whisper. "'Twere hardly a face at all."

"Did anyone hear anything?" Dr. Greystone asked after a moment, allowing the man a moment to grieve. "A scream or a struggle, perhaps?"

Hodgkin wiped his nose on the back of his hand. "No, I

don' belie'e so, sir," he muttered.

"Where is the nearest residence from this spot?" Dr. Greystone asked. "Do you know?"

Hodgkin nodded pensively. "'bout a five-minute walk from the other side of this 'ere valley live the Carnes. Brother and sister. Good people. 'Twas Carne's fiancé who first was killt."

"And you say no one heard a thing?" Agrippina verified.

"Not that I know, miss," Hodgkin replied.

"We should talk to the man who found her," Agrippina stated, scratching away at her notepad. "He is more apt to give us a first look at the scene."

"Agreed. I think we should talk to your daughter's fiancé next," Dr. Greystone said, turning to Hodgkin.

Mr. Hodgkin nodded. "Him a good lad. Missy loved 'im omething' dear."

"Come, let us move back to the carriage," Dr. Greystone said, ushering the defeated looking man back the way they came.

Agrippina hesitated for a moment and instead of walking with the men to the carriage she started to walk in the opposite direction, toward the middle of the valley. She stopped once she was satisfied with the distance and waited until the men were several seconds out of view around the bend.

She then took in a deep inhale and let out a blood-curdling scream. She stopped, listening as her voice reverberated back to her, its sound carrying on by the wind.

"Miss!" yelled Hodgkin as he came barreling around the path and straight up to her.

In her estimation, it took him twenty seconds to reach her.

"Miss, I thought that death 'ad come fer ya, fer sure!" Hodgkin panted having run all the way from around the bend to get to her. "What on earth got ya screamin' like a wil' banshee?"

"I was testing a theory," she stated calmly. "And it proved to be correct. The valley echoes."

Hodgkin looked at her like she was half mad.

"If anyone was around," her uncle explained coming up behind them slowly, "certainly they would have heard your daughter scream."

Hodgkin looked from one to the other, still trying to catch his breath. "And what would that 'ave to do wi' it?" he asked trying to follow. "If no one 'eard, there were no one 'round."

"Or, she did not have enough time to scream before she was attacked," Agrippina pointed out.

Drake Stan, the fiancé of the late Missy Hodgkin, was the son of the local cooper. Which is where Dr. Greystone and Agrippina found him, at his father's shop. Hodgkin, who had not been able to meet the eyes of the man who grieved as much over his daughter as he did, declined to join them for the interview.

The dusty blonde looked up from his work as they entered the shop, a tired look on his young face. "Can I 'elp you?" he asked politely, putting down his tools and wiping his hands on his apron.

"Are you Drake Stan, by chance?" Dr. Greystone asked.

"Aye, that be me," the young man replied, in a soft, but not timid voice.

Dr. Greystone introduced himself and his niece, explaining their business. Drake avoided eye contact for a moment at the mention of his dead fiancé's name, paling slightly.

"I thought that was all good and done wi'," he replied returning to his workstation. "The witch were caught, weren't she?"

"Is that what you believe?" Agrippina asked gently. "You believe that the killings are the cause of a witch controlling some hellhound?"

Drake shot her a sideways glance. "Don' rightfully know what I belie'e," he told her. "I only know that the kindest person I ever knowed is dead because o' it. Whether it be a witch or werewolf, or just a plain wolf, it ruined my 'appiness. That's what I knowed." He coughed. "That and there been no more killin's since that woman been caught. Though I 'ear you gone and freed 'er."

"Yes, well, we have reason to believe that it is not a witch or werewolf," Dr. Greystone explained. "At least those avenues should be searched before disregarded."

"You think it a wolf then?" he asked, picking up his sanding tool.

Dr. Greystone exchanged glances with his niece.

"No," she replied. "Wolves have been long extinct from Britain thanks to over hunting and the lack of respect for nature. We believe that it could potentially just be a man."

He blinked at her, confused. "You wouldna think it a man if ya saw the state o' my poor Missy," he told her, shaking his head slowly. "I don' know where you come from, but I know no man capable of such cruelty, miss." He put down the sander and cleared his throat. "She were unrecognizable." His voice shook with emotion and he swallowed audibly. "She were not my Missy." Drake sniffed as he spoke; his eyes staring off into the distance.

"Might you tell us about that day?" Agrippina asked as she turned to a new page in her notebook.

Drake hesitated but nodded. "She were s'pose to meet me at the tavern after she finished 'er work. But she never come. I wai'ed half a' hour a'fore I went lookin'. I thought she were jus' runnin' late and meetin' 'er on thee road would be a good surprise. But 'twas me who got the surprise." He shuddered as he said it, his doe eyes filling up with tears. "I saw 'er body layin' there an' no idea 'twas 'er. I didn' recognize 'er she was so covered in blood."

"How *did* you know it was her?" Agrippina asked him.

He sniffed. "She uh ribbon in 'er 'air I give 'er. Even in the dim light of me lantern I could see it. It were pale blue like 'er eyes, though most o' it were red from-" He cleared his throat and shook his head. "That's how I knew me sweet Missy were gone." He turned away, hiding his face while he recollected himself.

"Could you tell us what you could see before you found her body?" Agrippina pressed.

He didn't seem to understand the question. "Beg pardon, miss?"

"Did you notice anything on your way to the b- on your way to finding Missy Hodgkin?" she clarified.

Drake gave a slow, confused shake of the head.

"Did you not pass anyone on your way to her? Did you notice someone on the other end of the valley? A shadow? Footprints? Anything unusual?"

"No, miss, I saw nothin' but me Missy layin' there." He looked a little ashamed. "'Twas 'ard to see nothin' else. As far as footprints," he shook his head, "that path be a main road. There be too many feet that travel that path daily to notice a one."

Agrippina pressed her lips together and nodded.

"Did you hear anything?" her uncle broke in as he walked about the room making his observations.

"No, I dinna think so," he replied, trying to recall.

"Mr. Stan," Agrippina began slowly, "was Missy warm when you found her?"

Drake frowned.

"I do assume you held her in your arms or touched her when you found her," she went on. "There is no shame in it. You found a loved one dead on the ground; it is only natural to hold her close to you."

He averted his eyes for a moment.

"Was she warm?" Agrippina repeated.

"I wouldna say she were warm but she were not yet cold though the night 'ad a chill to it," he replied quietly. "I do remember that. I thought to meself- I were a lil angry, you see that she were makin' me walk out in thee cold. I were thinkin' to scold 'er fer makin' me come get 'er." He looked uncomfortable. "Seems awful now."

Dr. Greystone nodded sympathetically.

"I know it was dark and your lantern was not very bright, but how much blood-"

Dr. Greystone cleared his throat a little too loudly, causing Aggy to turn her attention to him and notice his cross look.

"Forgive us for our mode of questioning, Mr. Stan," Dr. Greystone began. "But the next questions, however awful they may seem, are very important. We do understand you have suffered a terrible shock, but it would help us a great deal to find your Missy's killer if you answered them, however awful they may seem."

Drake nodded.

"Did you notice, or could you see a lot of blood where you found her?" Dr. Greystone asked.

Mr. Stan paled. "She were covered in it!" he exclaimed a little angrily.

"We understand that, sir. What we mean is whether there was a fair amount on the ground where you found her," Dr. Greystone clarified gently.

Drake blinked for a moment as he thought before

nodding. "Aye, there was blood all over the ground. I remember the-" he choked on a sob for a moment, "I remember the poolin' of it. It seemed it were everywhere."

"Thank you, Mr. Stan," Dr. Greystone replied. "I know this has not been easy for you."

The young man nodded.

"One more thing," Agrippina chimed in. "Where did Miss Hodgkin work?"

"At the Mackland estate," said Drake. "She were a maid there."

"Mackland? Why does that name sound familiar?" Dr. Greystone asked to no one in particular.

"James Mackland. His sister Karen were the fifth victim," Drake clarified.

"YOU ARE CROSS WITH ME, UNCLE," AGRIPPINA STATED AS they left the cooper's shop.

"I am not cross," he replied, popping the collar of his jacket to protect his neck from the wind. "I just want you to use more caution and finesse when talking to these people. They have suffered great loss and pain. The last thing they want is to relive the horror of that loss; and the last thing they need is someone indelicately making them relive it."

Agrippina bowed her head a moment. "You are right. Forgive me," she said. "I have never been good at empathy."

"Perhaps, you could make it your new study," her uncle suggested. "It is important not to offend the people we are trying to retrieve information from. If we do, they may not talk to us at all and we might miss some vital information."

She nodded. "I understand."

Her uncle went into another coughing fit, the force of it so strong that he had to lean against the carriage to help hold himself up.

Agrippina placed a hand on her uncle's back in comfort. "Are you alright?" she asked, her voice heightened.

He nodded, his coughs subsiding, but his face looked pale.

"I do not like these coughing fits, uncle," Agrippina told him, concerned.

"I am all right," he told her breathlessly. He pulled a flask from his jacket and took a swig causing alarm to fall over his niece's face. He smiled. "It is only water. Fear not. Your uncle has yet to turn into the campus lush."

She nodded. "Shall we call it a day? We can see what Mrs. Bragg has for lunch and perhaps a nice tea would do you well. Anything to get out of this wind might help."

He shook his head. "I thank you for your concern, my dear, but I shall manage," he reassured her.

Agrippina nodded in obedience, but she did not look relieved. "Shall we continue onto Mr. Mackland's then?"

Dr. Greystone thought about it for a moment. "No, Mr. Hodgkin said that it is on the far end of town, the other side of that valley where his daughter was found, I believe he said. We can start there tomorrow, but for now, what do you think of all the victims being killed on a full moon? Do you think it significant?"

Agripinna shook her head. "I think it important in the sense that a full moon provides more light than the other phases. It certainly does not turn anyone into a monster."

Dr. Greystone chuckled. "Agreed." He cleared his throat. "Now, let us talk to the first victim's family. Which girl was that?"

"Hannah Marks," Agrippina said, having memorized the list. "Mr. Hodgkin said she lives not far from him. About a short ride from the local drinking establishment."

"Ah! A nice cold ale does sound good."

Agrippina lifted a brow at him. "I thought you were not going to turn into the campus lush?"

"You know, a drink once in a while will not hurt you, Aggy dear," her uncle replied laughingly, helping her into the carriage before getting in himself.

She shook her head. "I have seen how harmless it is for Professor Hartley," she pointed out. "One too many times, I have seen him stumble into his classroom and if it were not for me writing his lessons, he probably would have been fired a long time ago."

Her uncle nodded. "I always wonder why you have such a soft spot in your heart for that man." He leaned his head out the window and gave their driver the name of residence they wished to go.

"He is a sweet man, despite his issues," she explained as the carriage lurched forward. "And beyond that, when his brain is not diluted with alcohol, he is brilliant."

Dr. Greystone nodded. "You know, he came to me once, talking about you. I had the craziest notion he was asking me for your hand in marriage."

Aggy averted her gaze out the window.

"Agrippina?" her uncle said, his brows lifted.

She sighed. "He has asked me," she began, "more than once."

"More than once?" her uncle laughed.

"Yes, but I do not think he has asked me multiple times because he keeps trying and hoping I will eventually accept. Due to drink, I believe he just forgets he has already asked me, and I have already declined his previous offers."

Her uncle let out a laugh. "I cannot believe you have never told me!" he roared, still laughing.

"Well, I did not want to embarrass the man!" she told

him, half embarrassed herself. "I was trying to protect what dignity he still has left."

"And how long has this been going on?"

She sighed. "These two years at least."

Her uncle laughed again, causing himself to cough, though mildly this time. "Secrets, secrets," he uttered. "I wonder what else you could be keeping from me."

"Nothing, uncle, I promise!"

He reached out and patted her hand. "It is perfectly all right, my dear. You are allowed your privacy. There is no harm in secrets, even from your poor, old uncle."

They arrived at the shambled Marks's residence before the silence of the carriage ride became unbearable and they both emerged rather quickly, as if to escape something they were both hiding from one another, or to avoid an unwanted conversation.

A man and a woman emerged from the small house set closely apart from several others in the same condition. Tattered laundry hung from lines, blowing gently in the chilly wind, and young children played in a small creek that snaked parallel to the stone shacks, for they could hardly be called houses.

Dr. Greystone removed his hat and bowed. "Good day," he began. "I am looking for the Marks family."

"'Tis we," said the man a little standoffish, his broad shoulders puffed out and his arms crossed over his chest.

Dr. Greystone introduced himself and Agrippina.

"We know who ye are," the man said. "They say ye let the witch go. They say ye think she be innocent."

Dr. Greystone cleared his throat. "That is correct."

"Then how come there been no more killin's since she were captured?" he asked. "But now she be free, she'll do it again!"

"The last murder or death occurred less than two months ago," Agrippina pointed out.

They turned their heads sharply to look at her.

"Between the other killings there were three months," she continued. "There is still another month at least before there is another one."

Mr. and Mrs. Marks looked at her as if she had declared herself the murderer; their faces showing both anger and bewilderment.

"If you would please," Dr. Greystone began, turning their attention back to him, "we would like to ask you a few questions about your daughter. We hope very much to-"

"Go back to where e'er 'tis you come from," Mr. Marks told them in a low growl. "I'll answer nothin'."

"Mr. Marks, we understand your grief, but you must see we only want to help-"

"My grief?" he repeated angrily, his eyes sparkling with it. "What could ya know about my grief? 'ave you ever buried a child?"

"Yes," Dr. Greystone replied gently after a short pause.

Mr. Marks looked taken aback for a moment, though his anger did not abate.

"I buried a child and a wife within the same year," he continued. "My wife died during childbirth and my son followed not six months later."

Mr. Marks's expression remained unchanged, but his wife's softened.

"Now, I know what it is to bring up painful memories, but the questions you answer here could help us find the true reason behind these deaths," Dr. Greystone pleaded gently. "We wish only to help your family and the other families of these poor girls."

Mr. Marks's stare hardened. "I'll no ask ye again," he

replied coldly. "Leave." He turned and went back into the house while his wife lingered, looking unsure of what to do.

She opened her mouth as if she wanted to say something, but her husband angrily shouted for her to come into the house. She bowed her head and obeyed.

8

Dr. Greystone and Agrippina returned to their inn where a letter had been waiting for the latter. She seemed rather confused as to whom could be writing her, but readily took and opened it.

"Who is it from, then?" her uncle asked as Mrs. Bragg poured them tea.

Agrippina looked up from her letter and waited for the innkeeper to leave the room before answering. "It is from Thomas."

"Lord Beresford? Your next great relisher?"

She shot him an unamused look. "Yes, it seems he wrote this letter soon after we left which is why it arrived so quickly."

"And what does he wish?" he prodded stirring sugar into his tea.

"He is re-extending his invitation for us to visit him in London after this business has been concluded."

Her uncle lifted a brow as he brought his cup to his lips. "Is that all it says?"

Aggy pressed her lips together for a moment before

sighing. "He wishes that the two of us continue a corre-spondence for he has greatly missed my sardonic sense of humor and border-line abusive remarks." She frowned. "Are my remarks abusive?"

Her uncle lifted his brow and set his cup down, clear-ing his throat. "I believe he might be saying that in gest, my dear, for why would he want to continue—or resume, rather—an acquaintance that is abusive?"

She eyed him suspiciously.

He unsuccessfully struggled not to smile. "Fine. If I am to be honest, your mode of speaking is sometimes a little too truthful."

"Honesty is appreciated. People want to know the truth."

Her uncle coughed lightly. "People want to hear what they want to hear and sometimes that is the truth while other times it is a watered-down version of the truth. One you are not skilled in giving."

She gave a small harumph.

"Shall you write him back?"

She subtly shrugged as she placed the letter down and sat across from her uncle. "I suppose I could, though there is nothing new to report."

"I am going to go out on a limb here and assume he does not care whether you have something to report or not," he told her. "I daresay, Aggy, my girl, he would be happy if all you wrote him was a hello."

"Just a hello?" she repeated a little confused. "What a waste of paper that should be."

Her uncle sighed. "What I am trying to tell you is that—"

"Sir, and miss!" came the haggard voice of Bertie, who hobbled over to them with a smile.

"Bertie, you look remarkably better," Dr. Greystone told her, half surprised.

"Ye 'elped me, sir," she said inching closer. "Yer medicine and care did work." She bobbed her head for a moment. "I'm glad yer safe. I fretted when ye left."

"There is nothing to fear, Bertie." Dr. Greystone took another sip of his tea. "We have been well treated here."

Bertie shook her matted head still in need of a brush. "Nay, sir, there be danger. I see it," she whispered. "Different danger for ye than fer the miss." The old woman patted her chest before she turned her dark eyes onto Agrippina who watched as they misted over. "Had a dream, did I. Saw ye runnin' fer ye life. Chased ye were by thee devil." She shook her head. "But no one can outrun thee devil. Ye'll be bitten. Must take care. Must take care." The woman began to shake as her eyes rolled into the back of her head.

Agrippina jumped from her seat and caught the old woman just before she fell to the ground. "Uncle!" she shouted as she placed her gently on the floor.

But as soon as the seizing started, it stopped, and a calm rushed over Bertie whose eyes fluttered opened. Eyes that were now blue.

Agrippina gave a small gasp when she noticed the difference. She continued to stare back into the woman's eyes thinking she made a mistake, but she was certain; her eyes had been dark only moments before.

Her uncle bent over on the other side of the woman and checked her pulse before pressing his hand to her forehead to gauge her temperature.

"I did i' again, I s'pose."

"Did what again?" Dr. Greystone inquired confused. "Are you all right?"

"I seen another vision," she replied, her eyes still distant. She took in a deep breath and let it out slowly. "'Twas i' awful?" She took another long draw of air. "Forgive me, sir, if i' were."

"There, there, Bertie," Agrippina told her soothingly, the old woman's head resting on her lap. "Let us help you to bed."

"That be nice, miss," the old woman replied, her eyes already drooping with fatigue.

Agrippina and her uncle gently pulled the old woman up from the floor and helped her shuffle down the hall to the room the innkeeper had prepared for her. When she was nicely tucked away, Bertie peacefully began to snore.

The other two had little time to contemplate what had happened only moments before when Mrs. Bragg informed them that they had a visitor. Their surprise at having a visitor heightened when they saw who it was.

"Mrs. Marks!" Agrippina exclaimed when they returned to the parlor.

The woman looked a little shaken, but she tried to smile. "I must 'pologize fer me 'usband," she said meekly, wringing her hands. "'e's a good man, but losin' our Hannah has been tough on 'im." Her eyes filled with tears as she talked, but she blinked them away.

"There is nothing to forgive," Dr. Greystone replied graciously, offering her a handkerchief and ushering her to a seat.

"Might I pour you a cup of tea?" Agrippina asked her.

The woman shook her head a little too quickly, causing one of her tears to dislodge and roll down her cheek which she quickly wiped away. "I've only a few minutes. Me 'usband is gone to thee Rose Bud fer a drink. I need to be 'ome when 'e gets back."

They nodded understandingly.

"We 'ave five childers, you see," she began through her tears, "but Hannah were our soul. We love all o' them, we do, but our other childers be boys and none of them be so tender 'earted as our dear girl." She dabbed at her eyes, swollen from crying. "'Tis e'en more a shame, for she were soon to be wed."

"She had a fiancé?" Dr. Greystone asked.

Mrs. Marks nodded somberly. "Aye, I dinna overly approve of the man, but she were taken, to be sure."

"Who was she to wed?" Agrippina asked pulling out her notebook.

"Robert Carne. 'e be the gamekeeper for Mr. Mackland."

Agrippina and her uncle exchanged glances.

"It is rather strange how this Mr. Mackland keeps coming up," Aggy whispered to him.

He nodded knowingly. "Why is it you did not overly approve of Mr. Carne?"

"'e 'as a bit o' a temper, you see." Mrs. Marks sniffed. "I don' think 'e e'er hit Hannah, but 'e be the jealous kind. 'e didna like it when she talked to other men or if other men looked at 'er. I told 'er she should break i' off, but she loved 'im too much."

"Where was your daughter found, Mrs. Marks?" Agrippina asked softly.

"She were found on the farmstead. Mr. Thrasher's farm. She 'ad just not come 'ome one night. We didn' know what to do. Then, three days later, Ol' Man Thrasher found 'er lyin' in the creek on 'is farm. Said the cows were actin' strange." She took in a shaky breath and let it out slowly. "Our poor girl 'ad been rottin' away for three days 'fore she were found. Fer three days our girl were wastin' away, alone."

Agrippina hesitantly reached out and patted the woman's hand. "I am very sorry for your loss. I cannot imagine what that must feel like."

Mrs. Marks nodded and tried to smile through her tears.

"Thank you fer yer kind words, miss."

"I know this is difficult, and I do not wish to cause you pain, but might you be able to tell us anything about the condition of your daughter's body?" Agrippina squeezed the woman's hand gently.

She sniffed and shook her head. "I ne'er saw it. 'Twer my 'usband who went to verify. I ne'er seen 'im so struck as when 'e come 'ome from doin' so. He wouldna talk for hours after."

"Do you know where Hannah was or what she was doing the night she went missing?" Agrippina inquired.

Mrs. Marks frowned, seeming offended. "She weren't doin' nothin' amiss if that's what yer thinkin'! She were a good girl!"

"You misunderstand me," Agrippina calmly replied. "I mean, did you know whether she was with a friend, coming home from work, or anything of the sort?"

Mrs. Marks looked a little ashamed at her outburst. "I belie'e she might've been goin' to see Robert Carne and his sister, but I don' know." Mrs. Marks wiped her nose with the handkerchief.

"Might you be able to tell us where Mr. Thrasher lives?" Dr. Greystone asked.

"I can tell you where he lived, sir. Poor Ol' Thrasher died not too long after my Hannah did. Though natural." She gave another sniff and rose from her seat. "I should be goin'. If me 'usband finds out I were 'ere, 'e'd be rightly mad."

"Thank you, Mrs. Marks, for coming to talk to us," Dr. Greystone told her. "We are going to find who killed your daughter."

"Bless ye, sir," she choked out. "Bless ye both." She then gave a stiff curtsey and quickly walked out of the room.

"It has been a very bizarre day," Dr. Greystone murmured

as they watched Mrs. Marks leave.

Agrippina nodded, a strange sense of uneasiness growing inside of her.

9

Agrippina was plagued by strange dreams all night. So intense were her nightmares that when she woke up, her bed sheets were twisted and half fallen to the floor. Though she could not necessarily remember what she had dreamed about, she woke with a forceful jolt and sense of panic. She sat for a full five minutes to calm her pounding heart and sense of anxiety before she rose out of bed.

She stood, her body aching as if she didn't sleep at all. She wanted to return to bed and try again, but she could already tell by the light poking its way through the curtains that she had slept longer than usual. So, despite her desire to fall back into a deep sleep, she got dressed, put up her hair—at least halfway, as she could never be bothered to waste the time for an entire updo—and made her way downstairs.

Her uncle greeted her with a weak smile which told her he had about as much of a restful sleep as she did. He poured her a cup of tea, however, and handed her the plate of sausage.

"You slept rather late, my dear," he stated. "Are you well?"

Agrippina nodded. "I do not remember waking at all

during the night, yet I feel as if I have barely slept at all." She sipped her tea, grateful for its warmth. "You look pale again, uncle." She furrowed her brows in concern.

Dr. Greystone gave another weak smile. "I must confess, I do feel rather fatigued myself."

Agrippina frowned. "You should stay and get some rest. I do not like how you have looked lately. I fear you might be getting sick."

He sighed, still smiling. "I appreciate your concern for me, but I cannot let you go about town asking questions on your own."

"Yes," she replied sternly, "you can. You know I am more than capable. I have handled people far coarser than the people here."

He chuckled. "It is not that I think you uncapable. It is that investigating something as serious as murder can be very dangerous. What would I do if something happened to you? Why, your father would come back from the grave and haunt me if I allowed you to do something that got you hurt."

Agrippina gave him a cross look. "Now, uncle, you know that is impossible."

"Which part?"

"Papa is dead, and I do not believe in ghosts."

He shook his head. "One day, you shall find out that just because you do not believe in something does not mean it is not real."

Agrippina, if she were accustomed to such a gesture, almost smirked. "Are you saying you believe in ghosts, uncle?"

He shook his head. "As I have said before, some things cannot be explained by logic."

"Regardless," she persisted, "I promise to be extra careful, and I will report back everything I have learned. You know how I am, uncle. I am too stubborn to deny as I will be in a cross mood all morning and you will wish me gone anyway."

He laughed. "However true that might be, I am still hesitant. We are outsiders to these people, and it is quite evident they do not take kindly to such."

"Then I shall call upon Mr. Mackland," she suggested. "He is apparently a gentleman of some sort. He, at least, should not be so rough around the edges."

Just then, Mrs. Bragg came in to take their dirty plates away.

"I shall ask our hostess about him!" Agrippina proclaimed. "Mrs. Bragg, might you tell me what sort of man Mr. Mackland is? Is he a good man?"

"Oh, the Macklands 'ave always been good people, miss. 'Twas an awful shame what 'appened to poor Miss Mackland. She was as good to the people 'ere in Blindburn as if they was 'er own. Very charitable to the poor."

"And the brother?"

Mrs. Bragg nodded. "I've 'eard no 'arm of 'im. Though he does not venture out as much as 'is sister had done. 'e be more like you and the sir."

Agrippina glanced at her uncle for a moment. "How so?"

"Very learned. Was abroad for several years until just over a year past, after their father died. Now, that were a kind man. Never denied anyone work if 'e could."

Agrippina nodded. "So, I should have nothing to fear by visiting Mr. Mackland and asking him a few questions?"

Mrs. Bragg shook her head. "No, miss, I belie'e young Mr. Mackland to be just as kind if not a little more reserved than 'is father." She gave a small curtsey and left the room with her hands full of dishes.

"See, uncle!" she triumphed. "There is no need to stop our investigation. "You rest and compile theories based on what evidence we may already have, and I shall visit this Mr. Mackland whom we have already heard so much about."

Dr. Greystone hesitated, but finally relented. "Fine," he sighed. "But I expect you back in three hours or I shall come looking for you."

"Uncle, there is no need to worry. You can trust me."

"It is not you I do not trust, my dear," he told her. "It is everyone else." He bent over and pulled a large hunting knife from his boot causing Agrippina to look at him in shock. He offered it to her. "Take it."

"Uncle!" she exclaimed in surprise. "I have no need for it. What on earth do you suppose me to be doing?"

He looked at her in earnest. "Please, my dear," he pleaded with feeling. "It will make me feel a little better knowing you have something with which to defend yourself."

She hesitated a moment before nodding and taking the six-inch blade. She stared at it. She had no idea how to properly use it, but to make her uncle happy she slipped it into her boot and smiled, though a little uneasily.

"Thank you, Aggy my dear. I can rest a little easier now."

Agrippina gave her uncle a quick kiss on the forehead, reassuring him once again of her abilities to handle herself before going upstairs to prepare to leave. He watched her go, his heart half beating in trepidation at her leaving on her own, and the other half because he soon had to tell her what he could no longer hide.

THE CARRIAGE PULLED UP TO A LARGE, DARK, STONE ESTATE surrounded by hills on one side and flat grasslands on the other, the River Coquet just visible beyond. It was an aesthetically pleasing sight that Agrippina could not help but appreciate.

The driver helped her out of the carriage, and she stared for a moment at the slightly foreboding-looking building seemingly out of place in such a picturesque scene. She had not stepped too far from the carriage when the sound of barking shook her from her reverie, and she turned in alarm to find two very large dogs running at her.

She froze for a moment, a prickle of fear coursing over her skin as she watched the dogs get closer. She took a deep breath, however, and held her ground. When the dogs were close enough, she held up her hand and in a loud commanding voice, ordered the dogs to stop.

Confused by the stranger's authority, the dogs did stop, sitting on their massive haunches. Recognizing them as harmless and only curious creatures, Agrippina put her hand out for them to sniff which they readily and gently did.

"My apologies!" came the breathless voice of a man left in the wind by his dogs.

Agrippina looked up at him for a moment, registering his lack of a jacket and slightly unbuttoned shirt; his hair was almost black and his eyes were as gray as the ever-changing clouds in a stormy sky. Her breath caught in her chest and for reasons unknown to her, she felt herself blush.

"I assume these feral beasts belong to you?" she asked him, standing tall again.

He blinked at her a moment. "They are not feral, not quite. Irish Wolfhounds. The speckled one is Hubert and the grey one is Angeline."

She nodded, patting them both.

"You got them to stop for you," he finally acknowledged. "They are not dangerous, by any means, but they are very excitable. They hardly listen to me though, so I am rather impressed. My gamekeeper tells me I am not stern enough." He chuckled. "I actually bought Hubert from him not long ago. Fine dogs my gamekeeper has. He is a much better trainer. He can get his dogs to do anything. Though he usually uses them for hunting."

She caught herself staring into his large brown eyes again which was only to keep her from staring at his slightly exposed chest and the small patch of hair peeking out of his unbuttoned shirt. "I am here to see Mr. Mackland," she finally said, shaking off her embarrassment.

"Are you?" he asked, almost smirking. "Might I ask whom I have the pleasure of meeting?"

Agrippina was shocked that the half wild-looking man in front of her was the man she had come to see. She had not expected to see a gentleman, as he was said to be, in a state of undress running around as he was.

His smirk turned into a smile when he realized he had surprised her. "Not what you were expecting, I suppose?"

She cleared her throat. "I am Agrippina Greystone," she introduced herself. "I have come with my uncle, Doctor Greystone to investigate the mysterious deaths happening in your town."

The young man nodded. "Agrippina," he repeated. "That is a good name." He gave a nod of his head. "And were you?"

Aggy blinked at him for a moment. "I beg your pardon?"

"Born feet first?"

Aggy gave one of her seldom smiles. "Do you speak Greek, Mr. Mackland?"

"Very poorly, I can assure you." He smiled in reply.

The grin had yet to leave Aggy's face as they held each other's gaze.

After a moment, she cleared her throat, her countenance becoming grimmer. "I heard your sister was one of the unfortunate women," she began in her down-to-brass-tacks tone of voice.

He looked surprised at her change in tone. "Yes, she was," he replied. "Karen was a kind girl from what I knew of her."

Aggy must have looked confused for a moment causing him to explain his meaning.

"I have only returned maybe a little over year ago from nearly a decade abroad," he enlightened her. "My sister and I were only a few years apart in age, but I had not seen her since she was a child. I had only just begun to become reacquainted with her when she was savagely taken from me."

"I am very sorry to hear that."

He nodded and they fell into silence.

"I am very rude, Miss Greystone," he quickly said realizing they were still lurking outside. "Might I invite you in so we may talk? I am sure there is a fire going and the wind off these hills sometimes is rather unbearable."

She dipped her head. "Yes, please."

He ushered her in, and she was surprised that the inside of the house was not as dreary as it appeared outside. The hall was pleasantly and tastefully decorated, and the chandelier sparkled in the little sunlight that shone in from an upper window.

"This way, Miss Greystone," Mr. Mackland told her holding his arm out to direct her, Hubert and Angeline not far behind them. "The front parlor has the best lighting during this time of the day. Shall I order us some tea, or would you prefer a glass of brandy?"

"No, I thank you. I shall not take up too much of your time."

He nodded curtly. "Please have a look around. I am going to make myself more presentable." He bowed and left her alone with the dogs to wonder at the scene before her.

Agrippina walked the parlor slowly studying the large deer heads mounted on the walls and an entire stuffed fox staring at her from a corner. Squirrels, rabbits, boars, all of them looked back at her with their cold glass eyes from different angles around the room. But it was the wolf that held her attention more than anything. Its teeth were bare, and its posture made it look as if it were about to pounce on you at any moment.

She approached it slowly, observing the fine detail of it's mottled white and grey fur and admiring the sharpness of its teeth and claws. She would hate to run into such a creature in the wild.

"That was taken down by my three times great grandfather," Mr. Mackland said as he entered, tugging on the jacket he just donned. "It has been in that corner of this house for over a century. I used to be afraid of it as a child."

"I am sure most children would be. It is still a beautiful specimen."

He nodded. "Now, please tell me what I can help you with. I hear you have already set that poor old woman free." He shook his head. "We are good, kind people here in Blindburn but most of us lack the opportunity to educate ourselves and, therefore, superstition tends to rule."

"Then what excuse does the vicar have?"

Mr. Mackland chuckled. "You are quick with your opinions, I can tell."

She looked over at him for a moment before returning her gaze to the wolf, staring into its empty, golden eyes.

"Tell me," he began, "why is it just you here and not you and your uncle? I thought the two of you were doing this investigation together?"

"Word does travel fast here, does it not?"

He grinned. "That vicar you spoke of made a point to visit me the other day after your disgruntled meeting. You really seem to have gotten under his skin. Though, I imagine most women who open their mouths to speak might perturb him."

Agrippina's facial features lightened a moment. "I must admit, I enjoyed ruffling his feathers. Being ignorant because you lack education is forgivable but choosing to be so is not."

"I could not have said it better myself."

They met each other's eye again and for a moment, Agrippina was unsure where she should look. She cleared her throat in the confusion and shuffled to a different part of the room.

"Shall we begin?" she asked.

"Please."

"Your sister went missing the beginning of September, is that right?" she asked as she pulled out her little notebook.

He nodded. "September sixth. She was supposed to be taking a trip to Edinburgh to look at dresses for her wedding, but she never made it." He cleared his throat. "I would never have known she was missing if it were not for her fiancé."

Agrippina frowned. "She was engaged?"

He nodded with a sigh. "To the son of a local wealthy businessman. Marvin Hawkins. He lives a few miles out of town. She was supposed to go to his house and leave with her sister the next morning, but she never made it."

"When were you alerted to this?"

He took a moment to think. "Sometime around seven or eight that evening. She was a rather punctual person, so the Hawkins family thought it strange she did not arrive at the time she said she would. They waited another hour, but when there was no sign of her, they went looking. They only found her horse, its leg badly broken."

"And your sister?"

He swallowed hard. "We did not find her for another five

days. Her body was somewhere halfway between our house and the Hawkins's. It appeared she had been dragged under a tree in an open field. She was found by chance—by miracle really—by two children who had gone exploring through the tall grass." He shook his head as if in disbelief. "Her body and face were completely mangled." He gave a shudder. "I cannot imagine what she went through. She deserved so much better."

Agrippina took a deep breath and let it out slowly.

"What are you thinking?"

She blinked at him a moment, unused to such a question from anyone other than her uncle. "I am rather unsure, to be honest," she confessed rather easily, if not uncomfortably. "There is a lot to process, and I have yet to talk to two other families of victims." She frowned for a moment. "I heard your sister was well liked among the people of Blindburn."

He nodded, smiling in remembrance. "Yes, she was very charitable. People often came to her if they needed help or even advice. She was very levelheaded and understanding. She always seemed to know how to best solve a problem. I was very proud of her for that."

"You do not know of anyone who would want to hurt your sister, would you?"

"No!" he readily answered, almost angry. "As I said, she was well liked. Loved even."

She nodded. "The third victim Missy Hodgkin worked here, did she not?"

He bobbed his head. "That is right. My sister was very attached to the girl; she was extremely upset by her death."

She scratched away at her notepad. "Were there any troubles between her and anyone else in your employ?"

He took in a deep breath as he thought. "No complaints that I can think of. She seemed a very well-behaved young woman. She was always on time, very obedient. If there were any issues, they were not brought to my attention."

She made another note. "Is your gamekeeper at work today by chance?"

"Robert?" he asked with a nod. "Yes, I saw him earlier today."

"His fiancé was the first victim and I was wondering if I might be able to talk to him?"

Mr. Mackland bowed. "I can have him sent for right away." He walked to the far wall and rang the bell.

A half a minute later, a young woman hobbled into the room, her grizzled hair falling out from under her cap and her left leg dragging behind her.

"Aye, sir?" she asked, wiping her hands on her apron.

"Rebecca, might you have someone fetch your brother for me, please?" Mr. Mackland told her. "There is someone here who wishes to ask him some questions."

The young woman, who could only be defined as unattractive turned her gaze on Agrippina with curiosity. She gave an awkward bow after a second or two and left the room.

"Are you quite sure I cannot offer you anything?" Mr. Mackland asked her again. "I believe you might be here for some time."

She gave a small frown. "Excuse me?"

He motioned to the window, where dark clouds were beginning to form.

"Oh, no!" she muttered under her breath.

"We get random storms every now and again," he explained. "It should blow over soon enough."

She nodded, but the concern had yet to leave her face.

"Is something the matter?" he asked gently.

"No," she quickly responded, though she was worried her

uncle would think the worst if she did not return to the inn at a reasonable time.

"I am sure it will be nothing." He rang the bell again and a different servant girl answered. "Michelle, please prepare tea for my guest and me."

The old woman nodded and disappeared back out the hallway.

"There!" he proclaimed. "You cannot avoid it now."

She nodded but gave no verbal response.

"You said earlier you are investigating the deaths with your uncle," he began when the conversation dwindled.

"I did."

"Where is he?"

"Investigating other avenues," she lied.

He nodded. "He trusts you then to make decisions and hypotheses based on what you learn?"

She creased her brow a bit. "Of course, he does. He knows I would never make a judgment or presumption with little or no evidence, and understands I am able to make calculations and come to sound conclusions."

Mr. Mackland smiled broadly at her which made her uneasy as she was unsure what she had said to make him do so.

"Do I amuse you, sir?" she asked trying to hide that she felt a little offended.

"Yes, you do," he replied honestly. "But do not automatically think that is a terrible thing. I have just never heard a woman talk the way you do."

She regarded him for a moment.

"In other words, I find you," he hesitated to choose the right word, "intriguing."

Agrippina blinked. "I do not believe anyone has ever called me that."

"Well, though I might be the first to say it, I doubt I am the first the think it. I am convinced rather."

Agrippina was unsure of what to say and was relieved when Robert Carne walked through the door.

"Becky said ye wanted to see me, sir?" Robert, a young, rough-looking man said as he took off his old hat and bowed his head.

"Yes, Robert," Mr. Mackland replied, gesturing him to come further into the room. "You do not have hover by the door. Come, sit, warm yourself. I have ordered tea."

"Yer very kind, sir." Robert hesitantly took a seat as his clothes were dusty and the furniture was rather fine, but on Mr. Mackland's insistence, he finally sat.

"This woman, Miss Greystone, would like to ask you a few questions concerning Hannah Marks, Robert."

Robert blanched before turning red.

"She is hoping to find out who truly killed her and the other young women.

Please be respectful and answer her as best you can."

Robert silently nodded.

"Hello, Mr. Carne," Agrippina began. "I am Agrippina Greystone as Mr. Mackland said. I understand you and Hannah Marks were engaged to be married, is that correct?"

Robert cleared his throat. "We was," he almost muttered. "Though she broke it off."

Agrippina was taken aback. "She broke off your engagement?"

He nodded. "A week afore she were killt."

"Why?"

He sniffed. "She said I didn' treat 'er right, though I did worship the ground she walk on!" He shook his head.

There was a brief pause as the maid Michelle came back in with the tea and prepared everyone a cup.

"Why did she think you did not treat her right?" Agrippina asked as she stirred her tea. "Did you ever hit her?"

Anger flashed over Robert's face. "I'd ne'er do a thing to 'arm 'er! I loved that girl. I still do. She were pretty and kind and I knowed I were marrying better than what I's worth." He shook his head. "She were my whole world. The reason I woke wi' a smile every mornin'. And now, she's the reason my 'eart be broke."

"You were not angry that she called the wedding off?" Agrippina watched his reaction closely.

"Who wouldn' be?" He held his tea in his hands but didn't sip it; he only stared into the amber liquid. "I begged 'er fer days to take me back, but it were no use. She didn' want me."

"Where were you the day she went missing September of last year?"

"I were probably 'ere," Robert replied, sounding unsure. "I always be 'ere, more or less, miss."

She nodded as rain began to beat against the window-panes. She turned to see the dark clouds from earlier had turned the sky black.

"Huntin' might be no good tomorrow," Robert said as he watched the rain. "Dogs can' track the foxes as well in this rain."

Agrippina, for some reason, felt this statement was important and quickly jotted it down in her notebook.

Finally, the rain abated a little more than an hour later and without delay, Agrippina made her excuses to leave.

"You are to go then?" Mr. Mackland asked, sounding a little disappointed. "I was hoping to invite you to dinner."

"That is very kind of you, but I must be getting back to my

uncle. We have yet to meet with the physician who attended to the bodies and must make plans to do so." She retrieved her bonnet and tied it hastily around her chin.

"That would be Dr. Johns," Mr. Mackland informed her. "He is a family friend, though a little peculiar. I shall write to him and tell him to expect you. He hates surprises."

"That is very kind of you. If you could tell him, we shall be there tomorrow by ten in the morning that would be most helpful. Where is he located?"

"Just west of here in the town of Mackendon. He is the doctor to both towns really. Brilliant man but not very patient. He might not like being asked questions by a woman."

Agrippina took in a deep breath through her nose. "I have hardened myself to men like that, Mr. Mackland. It no longer bothers me as it once did, for I know they only dislike me because they feel threatened by me. Threatened because they fear I am smarter than them which I probably am."

He laughed lightly. "I have no doubt you are."

Agrippina thought she felt herself blush again and hastened her exit. "It was very nice to meet you, Mr. Mackland. I am sure I will have further questions for you." She gave a quick curtsey.

"Of course! My house is always open to you and your uncle. If I can make yours and his stay more comfortable you will let me know? I had thought to extend an invitation for you and him to stay here but-"

"That is very kind of you, but we never would have been able to accept. As you are too close to the investigation, it would have been inappropriate."

He nodded. "I see."

"Thank you again, sir, for you time." Agrippina gave another small curtsey to his bow and left the room, nodding to the servant who opened the door for her. She had not made it far from the front stoop, however, when she heard someone calling her.

"Miss Greystone, ma'am!"

Agrippina turned and saw the maid Rebecca Carne limping toward her, her gimp leg kicking up dust as she pulled it along "Yes?"

"I couldn' let ye leave without tellin' ye me suspicions," the young woman replied. "I did 'ear through gossip and rumors, mind ye, that the killin's could be connected to a fued we've goin' wi' the Scottish town just up thee way."

Agrippina furrowed her brows. "A feud?"

Rebecca Carne nodded. "Aye, ma'am, we been warrin' so long, we long fergot why we be warrin'. Though we ne'er ferget the hate."

"Hmm." Agrippina pondered what Rebecca said for a moment. "I am sure the rumors are nothing, but I shall look into it. Thank you, Miss Carne, for bringing it to my attention."

The woman smiled brightly, showing several missing teeth. "'Tis wonderful, you," she said motioning her head at Agrippina. "A woman in a position of a man, doin' the same job."

"Thank you. That is very kind of you to say." She gave a subtle close-lipped smile. "Do be careful at night, Miss Carne. Please make sure to never be walking alone."

"Aye, me brother always makes sure to walk wi' me 'ome. An' if 'e can', I've one of our dogs who ne'er lets me out 'is sight," she assured her. She turned and pointed to a black Irish Wolfhound, laying just off the drive in the grass. "That be Linus. Me brother trained 'im to protect me. I be safe, miss."

Agrippina nodded. "I have no doubt you are. Thank you

again for the lead. Good day."

And with that she was handed into the carriage. As it pulled away, she couldn't help but look back at the great, stone manor, her stomach fluttering to see that Mr. Mackland returned her gaze from the front parlor window.

THOUGH AGRIPPINA WAS WORRIED HER UNCLE WOULD HAVE been concerned with her having taken longer than she had promised, she found him comfortably asleep in a chair in his bedroom, an opened book resting in his lap.

She smiled as she left the room again, closing the door quietly. When she turned around to go back downstairs, she was surprised to see Bertie standing closely behind her. She jumped and pressed her hand against her chest.

"You were so quiet, Bertie, I did not hear you sneaking up the stairs. You gave me a little fright."

Bertie did not respond for a moment, her face blank and her eyes—her eyes were dark once again.

"Bertie?" Agrippina said softly taking a step back. "Are you all right?"

"Did ye meet 'im?" the old woman rasped, her eyes distant and unblinking.

"Meet who, Bertie?" Agrippina asked slowly.

"The Devil!"

Agrippina gasped at the old woman's outburst.

"The Devil be near, miss. Don' let 'im fool ye. 'e be cunnin'; 'e be unforgivin'. The Devil! The Devil!"

Agrippina stared in horror as the old woman suddenly jolted, her eyes returning to their shade of blue. She smiled at Agrippina, her rotting teeth crooked in her wrinkled mouth.

"Good af'ernoon, miss," she said pleasantly, as if what had just passed never happened. "Did ye 'ave uh pleasant day?"

10

Agrippina and her uncle were surprised to see the vicar let into the breakfast room the following morning while they ate, a grim look on his face.

"She has done it again," he said in greeting as he walked into the room.

"I beg your pardon, vicar?" Dr. Greystone responded, confused.

"There was another attack last night," he growled.

"Is someone dead?" Agrippina asked in concern.

"Luckily, the witch only sought the blood of a few sheep this time. Possibly because she was too weak to do otherwise!"

"If she were too weak, then how was she able to transform on a night when the moon was not full?" Agripinna lifted a brow, challenging him.

"Because the devil willed it. He gave her the strength!" Vicar Harmon preached. "Now, she has built her strength back up and will strike again! Soon, no doubt!"

"That is ridiculous!" Aggy proclaimed. "You will say anything that will twist this scenario into your narrative, will you not?"

Vicar Harmon turned his fiery eyes on her. "You, woman," he all but hissed, "shall learn your place and are to remain silent while I am talking!"

Agrippina stood from her chair, glowering. "Listen here, vicar," she began in an acidic tone, "I do not do this often, but, when necessary, I find my rank has its advantages. I, sir, am not just a woman, but a lady. My father was the ninth Earl of Ipswich."

The vicar looked taken aback.

"Oh, yes, I see you are surprised, for I do not dress so elegantly as the daughter of an earl would, but I am in fact of noble blood, and you *shall* show me respect or so help me God, I shall use my connections to send you to a vicarage in one of our forgotten colonies!"

The vicar blanched slightly while her uncle gave her a disapproving look.

"Miss, had I known—"

"You can call me Lady Greystone, vicar," she interrupted.

The vicar quickly changed his tune and bowed. "Lady Greystone, had I known, I would never have talked to you the way that I did, I graciously assure you."

"I am only assured of your complete lack of respect for your fellow man or woman, sir," she stated. "You are a vicar and are supposed to be a bodily representation of our lord and savior here on earth, and, yet, you only have regard for people of rank? You disappoint me beyond belief." Agrippina gave a dismissive nod of the head.

Dr. Greystone cleared his throat and shot his niece a questionable glance. "Do go on about the sheep, vicar."

The vicar looked unsure of what to say as his conviction had been shaken by Agrippina's declaration. "There were two sheep butchered, much like the young women, found this morning. Something got into their pen last night and mutilated the poor creatures." He cleared his throat. "Forgive me for the language, my lady." He gave a slight bow.

"Did you say something got into the pen?" Agrippina asked.

The vicar nodded. "Yes, Lady Greystone, they had all been tucked away for the night."

"That is rather strange," she bemused. "Pens are meant to keep other animals out. How should one have gotten in?"

"The farmer said the gate had been wide open," the vicar explained. "It appears one of his hands forgot to close it the night before."

"Or someone opened it for the beast," Aggy whispered.

The vicar cleared his throat after a moment. "At any rate, the people are asking that the wretched old woman be taken back into custody for the safety of its young women."

Dr. Greystone shook his head. "Bertie shall remain here under our watch. If you insist she is the witch who has brought about the beast, then we shall be sure to lock her door at night to prevent another event such as this, but we will not release her into the inhumane conditions in which we first met her."

Vicar Harmon looked disappointed and a little angry, though this time he held his tongue. "I will relay what you have said to those concerned, but I cannot guarantee their satisfaction."

"What is life without a little disappointment?" Dr. Greystone told him.

"I could not agree more with you, sir." He bowed stiffly, forcing a smile.

The vicar left soon after this interview and when he was gone, Dr. Greystone was quick in scolding his niece.

"Did you have to tell him all of that?" he asked her a little crossly.

"I know! We are not one for bragging, but I felt rather justified. Did you see the way he changed his tone when I told him?" she shook her head. "It is disgraceful. I did it more to prove a point than anything."

"You hate being called 'Lady Greystone.'"

She made a face. "That is true, but it still served its purpose."

"You also hate people treating you as such just because of our rank."

"Yes, well, as the vicar would probably agree, some people just need to be reminded of their place, uncle," she stated with certainty. "And that man is one of them."

Her uncle took in a deep breath and let it out slowly. "I cannot deny your reasoning, my dear, but I still do not agree with it." He tapped the table with his fingers in slight agitation.

"Well, if anything, I think it saved Bertie from more persecution for now," she pointed out, watching his fingers twitch.

He nodded. "You are right. At least we have spared her another day in that hell."

By luck, the farm where the sheep had been slaughtered was on the way to Dr. Johns' and they made it a point to stop by to see if there was anything left to investigate. The farmer, out of fear and superstition they found, had yet to dispose of the bodies.

Flies buzzed as the smell of raw innards filled the air and Agrippina coughed to keep herself from gagging. She pulled her handkerchief out and pressed the scented fabric against her nose and mouth.

"Found them a little after sunrise," the farmer, a rough-looking man in his forties told them.

Agrippina swallowed her nausea as she gazed upon the unfortunate animals. Something did not seem right to her, but her head was so clouded by the grotesqueness of the scene, she was unable to figure out exactly what it was.

"You say the gate was opened, Mr. Thorn?" Dr. Greystone asked bending over to look at the creature more closely.

"Aye, sir," he replied. "It was banging slightly in the wind. I heard it before I saw it." The man nodded as he remembered. "The other sheep were mewing pretty loud too. I could tell they were spooked."

"Is it just the two?" Agrippina asked, peering over her handkerchief.

Mr. Thorn nodded. "Aye, I counted twice and only these two were unaccounted for."

"Hmm." Dr. Greystone stood and moved about the area, searching the ground. "Did you find any animal tracks?"

The farmer shook his head. "None that I could tell. The pen is all grass. No dirt to leave a mark in."

Agrippina moved closer to the gate opening, examining the ground. She frowned a moment. "What are these?" she asked, pointing to small drag marks leading away from the enclosure.

"I don't know, miss," Mr. Thorn replied coming over to look at what she was referring to. "I suppose they could be from the beast dragging my sheep away."

She shook her head. "No, there is not enough mud caked into the sheep's wool," she pointed out. "If the animals were dragged, there would be more than blood staining them. These poor things were killed and died where they fell."

The drag marks were not consistent and each one was met with a small break before it began again. She took note of them, but they soon fell into insignificance as her uncle informed her they had to go.

They had an appointment to keep with the doctor.

"There was something strange about that scene, uncle," Agrippina stated as they rode to the doctor's. She frowned in mild frustration, unable to discern what it was that had been so out of place.

"And what was that, Aggy?"

She sighed and shook her head. "I cannot figure it out."

"Oh, dear," Dr. Greystone said with a subtle smile. "Should I leave you to figure it out before we meet with the doctor?"

"Why should you say that?"

He laughed. "You are never more formidable, my dear, than when you are unable to figure something out."

"That cannot be true!"

"I most heartily assure you it is," he chuckled. "I remember when you were learning the harpsicord—or demanding to be taught, as your several tutors would say."

Agrippina narrowed her eyes at her uncle.

"Anyway, you could not figure out a piece by some composer or another and for a week while you practiced, the entire house staff avoided you because you were so dreadful." He laughed again as he remembered. "There have been other times, but that is the one I remember the most fondly. For days you locked yourself in that room only coming out to eat or sleep. You did not quit until you had the song committed to perfect memory."

Agrippina, as usual, was not amused by her uncle making her the butt of his joke. "Well, had that behavior been brought to my attention earlier, perhaps, I could have corrected it."

Dr. Greystone shook his head. "Absolutely not!" he exclaimed. "I would not have changed that about you for the world. It is that drive to do better and know more that makes you the woman you are today. You never give up and that is to be admired."

"A compliment now? I suppose I should thank you."

He patted her hand. "Mull it over, child," he told her. "You will figure it out soon enough, I am sure."

They arrived at Doctor Johns's small cottage a little after their appointed time but were greeted with warmth by the housekeeper and ushered into the Doctor's study. Agrippina looked in interest at the jarred specimens that lined the walls. It reminded her of her uncle's office in Oxford.

She took a step closer to one of the large jars and stared at it. Looking into the eyes of the strange, preserved creature, long dead, floating in the murky liquid.

"That is an anaconda from the Amazon," came a steady voice from behind them.

"Yes, and quite young," Agrippina added as she turned and met the eyes of Doctor Johns. "I am told they can grow monstrously large."

He sized her up for a moment before giving a smiling nod. "That is correct." He walked to his desk by the window. "I was informed by Mr. Mackland you would be coming to see me at ten. You are rather late."

"That is my fault, Dr. Johns," Dr. Greystone said. "I insisted on stopping at Mr. Thorn's farm first. Two of his sheep were attacked and killed last night supposedly in the same manner as the young women."

He nodded. "Most unfortunate what those poor young women went through." He sighed. "I tended to them all. Even poor Miss Mackland whom I also helped bring into this world. It was strange to see her after she had departed. Especially since I am an old man compared to her. It should have been the other way around. She was a kind girl."

The Greystones nodded.

"We have heard wonderful things about the young woman," Dr. Greystone replied. "It seems she was well liked."

"That she was." Dr. Johns nodded. "Now, James informed me that you had some questions you might like to ask."

"That would be Mr. Mackland, I presume," Agrippina said.

Dr. Johns nodded. "I brought all the Mackland children into the world. All five, now there are only two left. Mr. Mackland you know, the eldest girl married a few years ago, the other three died." He shook his head. "Sad business. James has had a difficult life, despite the riches he may possess."

There was a brief silence.

"Ah, sorry, I know I have a habit of digressing. If my beautiful wife were still alive, she would have laughed at me." Dr. Johns rummaged through some papers on his desk and picked up a large leatherbound notebook. "Now, ask away!"

"What is your opinion on the wounds, Doctor?" Dr. Greystone asked clearing his throat.

"It is a strange business," the slightly younger man replied. "The young women were all cut in the same way; deep penetrating wounds while still alive."

The Greystones waited for him to elaborate but he just sat there bobbing his head.

"What kind of wounds were they? Were they slashes, stabs, or cuts?" Agrippina offered in assistance.

"Oh, yes, slashes indeed," he replied. "Mostly in the face and torso area. A few on the arms and legs as it was evident the poor wretches fought for their lives."

"Might I see your notes taken during the autopsies?" Agrippina asked.

The doctor eyed her skeptically. "I do not believe I can in good conscience let you see them, young lady," he replied.

"The details are too graphic, and I would much rather not be responsible for one of your swoons."

Dr. Greystone coughed to keep from laughing and turned his attention to a butterfly display on the wall to avoid eye contact with his niece.

"I can assure you, sir," she began a little bitterly, "I have never swooned in the twenty-two years of my existence, and I have dealt with far worse than a few slashes."

The two of them held an equally stubborn glance, but the doctor's curiosity gave out at last.

"All right then, very well," he replied with a shrug as he handed her the large notebook from his desk. "Though I am not sure what you will find in them that I cannot tell you myself."

Agrippina resisted the urge to huff as she picked up the leather notebook and opened it. She marveled at the detailed drawings the doctor made of the young women, impressed with his way of detailing where the wounds were, how deep, and how long. After a moment, she frowned.

"No one mentioned a bite mark before," she stated without looking up, interrupting the doctor's explanation to her uncle's inquiry about his bug collection.

Dr. Johns cleared his throat a little annoyed. "Ah, yes, the bite mark," he said. "They all had them. Just one, around the throat."

Agrippina looked up at her uncle, her brows slightly furrowed. "Could you make out what kind of a bite mark it was, or at least, do you think you have a guess as to what made the bite mark?"

The doctor shrugged. "I cannot pretend to be an expert on teeth, but I am rather convinced it was some sort of an animal. The wound was deep, caused by large, sharp canines. It was a ripping wound, nothing like a human could have done, I am sure."

"And the wounds? Would you say they were clean?" Agrippina asked.

The doctor looked at her confused. "What do you mean?"

"I do not see anything in here noting what you found *in* the wounds. Dirt, debris, bugs." Agrippina flipped through the notebook and shook her head.

"If you turn to the notes I have for Missy Hodgkin and Francine Mellows, you will see my notations on the cleanliness of the wounds. For the most part, they were free from debris," the doctor told her. "Obviously there was bug activity in the women who were not found right away. But, for the Hodgkin and Mellows girls, their wounds were clean."

"Clean?" Dr. Greystone repeated. "How is that possible?" He walked over to his niece and looked over her shoulder as she read through the notebook. "Why would there not be any debris or dirt if they were attacked by an animal? That is rather curious."

Dr. Johns shrugged. "I could not think of a reason."

Agrippina's frown deepened as she realized what it was that had been bothering her about the sheep. "Were there any signs of chewing, tearing or eating of the bodies?"

Dr. Johns blinked at her. "No, other than some scavengers on the women not found right away. But, again, Miss Hodgkin and Miss Mellows were found within hours or less of their death. There were only the slashes and the bite mark."

Agrippina gave an astonished look at her uncle. "Clean wounds, no signs of eating. Does that not sound rather strange of an animal attack?"

Dr. Johns nodded. "Yes, I suppose it does."

Agrippina shook her head, a satisfied smile on her head.

Her uncle knew that look; she had just proved herself

correct.

"Is there anything else I can help you with?" Dr. Johns asked them.

Agrippina and her uncle shook their heads almost in unison.

"I do not believe we have any more questions, but might I borrow your notebook?" she pleaded. "I will have it copied by tomorrow and have it sent back."

The man hesitated but nodded. "If you think it will help you with the investigation."

"It already has," she triumphed.

AGRIPPINA'S SMILE DID NOT FADE BY THE TIME SHE AND HER uncle made it into the carriage.

"Alright, out with it," Dr. Greystone said, a brow raised as he handed his niece back into the carriage. "I know that look of yours. What have you come up with?"

"Well, it started with the sheep," she began. "I am rather glad you made us stop there first because seeing their poor bodies in that state helped me visualize what I needed to know."

"Go on?"

"If an animal had broken into the sheep's pen and killed two sheep, why is it they had not been eaten? Why is it their wounds were so clean?"

He smirked. "I know the answer, but I would much rather you tell me. I love to see you so worked up."

"Uncle, the lack of dirt and debris in the wounds has convinced me more and more that these crimes were not committed by an animal but by a man. If it were a beast of some kind, then the wounds would be littered with dirt and leaves and all manner of filth. Dirty paws would leave dirty wounds."

Her uncle nodded.

"Not only that, but the bodies were left intact! Animals do not tend to kill for sport; they kill for food. So why waste the energy if you are not going to eat your prey?" She shook her head. "Nothing else makes sense."

Dr. Greystone gave a satisfied sigh. "I am in total agreement with you, on everything except for one thing."

Agrippina gave a confused look at her uncle. "And what is that?"

"The bite mark," he told her. "What do you make of that?"

She blinked for a moment, thinking. "I do not know yet." She frowned. "That is the one thing that does not fit my puzzle."

He patted her hand. "All in good time," he told her. "I am sure you will figure it out soon enough."

The carriage lurched along the path back to the inn, and somewhere nearby, a dog barked.

11

THE GREYSTONES WERE SURPRISED TO FIND MR. MACKLAND waiting for them upon their return, sitting and chatting with Mrs. Bragg. She blushed and giggled as he told her stories about his travels on the continent all the while serving him tea and biscuits.

They both stood in surprise when the Greystones entered as if they had never expected them to come. Mr. Mackland bowed as Mrs. Bragg moved to make room for them at the table.

"I'd not expect ye back so soon, sir, honest! Or I'd 'ave—"

"It is alright, Mrs. Bragg," Dr. Greystone assured her. "You are allowed to entertain in your own home. Please sit and enjoy your tea."

"Very kind of you, sir," Mrs. Bragg said a little hesitantly as she sat back down and grabbed another one of her little cakes.

"Mr. Mackland, it is nice seeing you again," Agrippina stated.

Mr. Mackland bowed again, a slight smile on his face. "Miss Greystone. Mrs. Bragg informed me you have just been to see the doctor. I hope he was of sufficient help."

"Of course." She turned to her uncle. "Uncle, this is Mr. Mackland."

The two men bowed at each other.

"I am rather glad the two of you have come to help us," Mr. Mackland confessed. "When I wrote that letter to Lord Helston, I honestly did not think he would care to respond. My father and he were friends at school, but I know we are far from the eyes of London and, therefore, are of little consequence."

"Well, I must say I was rather intrigued when the opportunity arose, but it was my niece who was the main driving force on getting us here." Dr. Greystone nodded at Agrippina.

"I would not have doubted it after meeting her. Miss Greystone is quite formidable." His smile deepened.

Dr. Greystone chuckled. "Careful, young man, my niece does not take well to teasing."

Agrippina cleared her throat. "Might I inquire why you are here, sir?" she asked Mr. Mackland. "Do you have some new information for us? Something you remembered?"

Mr. Mackland looked at little embarrassed. "I must confess, I called to ask the both of you to dinner tonight."

Agrippina looked taken aback, while her uncle was only pleasantly surprised.

"Though I am sure my cook has nothing on Mrs. Bragg here, I thought it would be nice to give her the night off."

Mrs. Bragg giggled, a strange sound coming from someone her age.

Agrippina stammered a moment. "W-well, that is very—I do not think—"

"What a refreshing idea, Mr. Mackland!" her uncle proclaimed, stopping her from declining his invitation. "I do apologize for not having met with you yesterday, but my niece told me all about it. Right down to the Irish Wolfhounds threatening to eat her."

"That is an exaggeration, uncle," Agrippina said softly.

Her uncle waved her off lightly. "Agrippina had such a dog growing up. Atlas was his name, for that was one of her favorite Greek myths. Anyway, blasted dog would follow her around the house and knock everything off tables and displays with its tail." He laughed. "He was rather lovable though."

Mr. Mackland regarded Agrippina, noting her embarrassed annoyance. "I would love to hear more of these stories over dinner. Perhaps, I can persuade you to buy another dog such as your Atlas as I am breeding mine."

"Oh, heavens, no! Our housekeeper might turn us out. She is a rather cross old woman who has been with me since I was a boy, and I would not dare go against her."

Mr. Mackland laughed.

"At any rate, sir, I am verily looking forward to dinner."

Mr. Mackland bowed. "I am glad to hear it." He turned to Agrippina, his dark eyes smiling. "Good day, Miss Greystone."

She gave a half curtsey in response. "Mr. Mackland."

Dr. Greystone eyed his niece as Mrs. Bragg ushered their guest out, a smile on his face.

"What?" Agrippina inquired impatiently, half glaring at her uncle.

"I believe you have another relisher."

"Do not be ridiculous," she told him. "He is only being civil as we are investigating the untimely death of his poor sister."

"I am sure that is part of it, but it is not all of it."

"Uncle, not every young man who looks in my direction is interested in me."

"They would be if they were smart," he replied with a nod, "or had even half a brain for that matter. You are worth being interested in, my dear."

She laughed through her nose. "I do not doubt the latter part of your statement, but that does not mean a man interested in me is worth being interested in himself."

He sighed, smiling somberly. "I just want you to be well looked after when I am gone," he told her.

She creased her brows. "I am sure I shall be fine regardless, uncle. Besides the inheritance I am to receive, I am capable of managing myself."

"Yes, but I do not wish you to be lonely as—" He shook his head. "Never mind, for now. But I do wish you would consider returning the interest of some young man. Perhaps Lord Beresford would do well."

"Not Professor Hartley, then?"

Dr. Greystone smirked. "Was that a joke, my dear?" he asked, amused.

"Yes, uncle, for I am as serious about marrying Professor Hartley as I am marrying any young man."

Dr. Greystone shook his head. "I do not know why, Aggy dearest, you are so set against marriage. You came close once, did you not?"

Agrippina's face flashed red at the remembrance. "No," she quickly and defensively replied. "I would not call whatever attachment there might have been between me and Mr. Willards as *close* to anything." She cleared her throat. "At any rate, I will never let myself be fooled by a man again." She stood and made her way to the door. "Excuse me, but I think I shall like to freshen up. And then, perhaps after lunch, we could visit the family of Francine Mellows before we go to dinner at Mr. Mackland's."

Her uncle nodded.

"It is important to stay on track, uncle, as you have always told me. The young often give way to distractions."

He watched his niece go with a sigh. "Some distractions are worth giving way to, my dear," he said to no one as she had already left the room.

FRANKLIN MELLOWS SOBBED WHEN DR. GREYSTONE AND Agrippina introduced themselves, ushering them into the small house.

"Forgive me, sir an' miss," he mumbled into an old rag. "I've not talked 'bout me poor Francy for months now. 'Tis too painful."

"We are, by no means, here to cause you pain, Mr. Mellows," Dr. Greystone told him gently. "We are merely here to find out who did this to your daughter and the other young women."

"'Twas that witch!" came an angry male voice from the door.

The Greystones turned to find a tall young man leering at them.

"'Twas that ol' witch and yous let 'er go," he growled. "Now she be free to kill again!"

"You hush yer blasted mouth!" Mr. Mellows yelled. "Now you go out back an' tend to yer sisters. I'll 'ave no more yellin' while we've comp'ny."

The young man glowered at Dr. Greystone and Agrippina but did as his father bid him and stormed out the back door, slamming it behind him.

"You must forgive me son Harold," Mr. Mellows said. "'e not only lost 'is sister to the beast, but 'is fiancé as well. Georgina Wilkes was 'is girl."

"The fourth victim was your son's intended?" Agrippina

clarified.

"Aye, miss. Me son built a 'ouse fer them just next to thee blacksmith shop where 'e were goin' to work." He shook his head. "But after losin' 'is sister and 'is love, 'e got lost in drink. I canna bring 'im back. 'e mourns sum'in great." He began to sob again. "I've five more girls, ye see," he said quietly. "And I'm afeared of what the beast can do to 'em." He sniffed and wiped his nose on the back of his sleeve.

"Was your daughter due to be married as well, Mr. Mellows?" Dr. Greystone asked already knowing the answer.

The man nodded. "Aye, to Sam Higgins. He were a good man. Loved Francy sum'in fierce."

"Were?" Agrippina repeated, picking up on the past tense. "Is Mr. Higgins no more?"

"Aye, poor lad," Mr. Mellows replied. "I ne'er seen someone so struck wi' grief a'fore. He couldna bear to live wi'out me sweet lass, so he throwed himself in the coquet."

"In the river?" Dr. Greystone clarified.

"Aye, sir. Drowned 'imself, 'e did." He shook his head at the thought of the wasted life.

"Do you know what your daughter was doing the day she was attacked?" Agrippina asked gently, keeping them on track.

Mr. Mellows cleared his throat a moment as he thought. "She were visitin' a friend, I belie'e." He nodded. "Aye, she were visitin' the Carne girl, Rebecca."

Agrippina tilted her head inquiringly. "Mr. Mackland's maid?"

He nodded again. "Aye, she's the one. She's a bad leg. Club foot, or of the like. Had a terrible time o' it growin' up. Poor girl were always teased. But me dear girl Francy always stood by 'er, 'elped 'er, she did." He sniffed and paused to compose himself. "She went to visit due to Rebecca bein' in pain, an' needin' soothin', so me girl brought 'er a salve she made to 'elp ease her friend's pain an' give 'er sum'in to 'elp 'er sleep."

"She sounds like a lovely, kind girl," Dr. Greystone said in a soft tone.

Mr. Mellows buried his face in his hands and cried, his shoulders shaking. "She were the best daugh'er I could've asked for, sir," he said through his tears. "I ne'er deserved 'er. She were too good, too kind."

Agrippina felt uneasy. All the women so far had some sort of connection to Mr. Mackland or his household, and she had yet to decide if this was pure coincidence or whether she should begin to suspect something more.

"Am I to believe, Mr. Mellows, that Georgina Wilkes lived nearby?" Dr. Greystone asked when they were done with their interview. "I was told she did."

Mr. Mellows nodded. "Aye, she grew up wi' me daugh-ter an' me son. Wilkes' be the 'ouse wi' thee red door." He cleared his throat and sat up straighter in his seat. "I do bless ye, sir, an' miss. And I pray ye find thee true killer. I ne'er liked thee ol' woman fer it. Though me son be too 'urt to agree, she ne'er caused pain to no one."

"Ye forget, father, the time ol' Bertie slapped Hannah Marks and cursed 'er," Mr. Mellows's son said from the door-way. He narrowed his eyes at the three of them.

"Cursed her?" Agrippina said skeptically.

"Aye!" Harold turned his eyes on her. "Left three scratch marks on 'er face." He held up three fingers and raked them across his cheek. "Then spat on thee ground and mum-bled under 'er breath. 'Twas a curse. Not long after, Hannah were dead!"

Mr. Mellows scoffed. "That Hannah Marks were a mean girl!" he yelled. "She were nice to yer face and to the fancy folk, but she felt little amongst 'er own people. She were always pickin' on those she thought 'neath 'er just 'cause she work fer the Macklands. She thought she were sum'in special."

"Hannah was mean to Bertie?" Dr. Greystone asked.

Mr. Mellows looked a little uncomfortable, almost apologetic. "Aye, I noticed it meself. She of'en threw things at thee poor ol' woman, made fun o' 'er, though she were always nice to e'eryone." He shook his head. "A lot o' the kids do it now. Not all parents stop 'em, but if I e'er saw my childers pickin' on a poor old maid- well, they knowed not to do it again."

"Thank you very much for your time, Mr. Mellows, and Mr. Mellows," Dr. Greystone said with a bow. "You have been very helpful."

Agrippina gave a small curtsey.

"Aye, whate'er I can do to 'elp," Mr. Mellows replied. "I wish I could do more, but I only knows what I knows."

Harold scoffed earning a glare from his father.

"Good day to you both."

Another bow, and Dr. Greystone and Agrippina left, their minds full of questions.

"They were all engaged, uncle," Agrippina stated. "Does that not seem strange to you?"

He nodded. "It is by no means extraordinary as they were all of marrying age, but it certainly would be a rather big coincidence if it did not mean anything."

Agrippina took a deep breath and let it out slowly, all the while looking for the red door of the Wilkes's. "Five women murdered, four of them from the working class; one of them from the genteel class. The one thing they all had in common besides their gender was they were all soon to be wed."

"Except Hannah Marks."

She nodded. "You are quite right. She had broken her engagement off prior to her murder. But what if the murderer did not know that? Mrs. Marks told us herself that her daughter was engaged to Robert Carne. She had not told us they broke the engagement off. Robert was the one who told me."

Her uncle nodded. "Could Robert have done it because he was angry?"

She pondered the thought for a moment. "I am not sure. It is possible, but he seemed rather distraught when talking about her death. And even if he did kill her, why the other killings? Why not just kill her and be done with it? If only the two of them knew the engagement had been broken off, there would be less suspicion as there would have been no motive."

Her uncle smiled pensively. "I love the way your mind works."

"Uncle Al, be serious."

"I am serious, my dear!" he proclaimed. "Your mind is rather fascinating. I am prodigiously proud of you."

"Thank you," she replied with a nod. "Oh, I believe that house must be the Wilkes's." She pointed to a ramshackle little home with a red door in contrast to the other bland brown ones of their neighbors.

Their knock was met by a timid looking man in his forties, followed by his wife, a petite woman with greying hair.

"Can we 'elp you?" the man asked suspiciously.

Dr. Greystone stated their purpose to which Mr. Wilkes opened the door to his house just enough for Agrippina and Dr. Greystone to squeeze in sideways.

"Thank you, sir, and, ma'am, for allowing us into your home. We know this whole ordeal must be very difficult."

The two of them nodded silently.

"We will just ask you a few questions and be on our way," Dr. Greystone explained.

Again, the couple nodded.

"Could you please tell us about your daughter's last day alive?"

The wife, Mrs. Wilkes, looked away, the wound still raw.

Mr. Wilkes merely sniffed and swallowed hard. "It were a day like any other, if I can recall. Nothin' special. She went to work at Mr. Thorn's farm as she always did. She 'elped take care o' the sheep. It might 'ave been a sheerin' day 'cause she left 'ome early, come 'ome real quick after work to grab sum'in, left, an' jus' didn' come 'ome."

"Was that unlike her? To just not come home?" Agrippina asked.

The two of them stared at her, different levels of shock plastered on their faces.

"She were not the type to go messin' 'round if that what you mean," Mrs. Wilkes asked, offended.

"No, ma'am, not at all," Agrippina replied in defense. "I was wondering whether she sometimes stopped at a friend's first before coming home or not."

Mrs. Wilkes nodded after a moment. "Aye, sometimes she would stop by at the Mellows's, especially after what 'appened to Francy. They was the best o' friends, ye see. They did e'erythin' together. And, then when Harold and 'er became engaged, why they was both so 'appy to call each other sister." Tears welled in the woman's eyes, and she paused a moment to compose herself. "But she were always back to sleep in 'er own bed. She knew better than to keep us worryin' like that."

"So, that day, she was to leave for work and return home directly?" Dr. Greystone asked.

Mr. Wilkes shook his head. "No, she did return, but only

fer a few minutes. She were to drop off a scarf she 'ad made to Mrs. Thrasher whose 'usband died not long a'fore an' came 'ome to retrieve it first." He nodded, racking his brain about the details of that day.

"Do you know if she made it to Mrs. Thrasher's?" Agrippina inquired, jotting down the information.

Mrs. Wilkes shook her head. "No, I don' belie'e she e'er made it. Scarf were still on 'er when she were found four days later." She smiled weakly, her lips trembling. "I can still see 'er sittin' o'er there in the window knittin' it. It were such a pretty shade o' blue, but when we found 'er," she pressed a shaking hand over her chest as her eyes welled with tears, "how stained it were with 'er–" She looked away, unable to finish her thought.

Mr. Wilkes cleared his throat and ran his hands through his fair hair. "She were on 'er way to doin' sum'in kind, and that 'appens to 'er." He shook his head. "It don' make no sense."

"It never does," Dr. Greystone replied in sympathy.

"Georgina was our last remaining child," Mr. Wilkes stated quietly. "All the others gone too. All five of our childers." His lip quivered. "Dead a'fore us."

"We be thinkin' of leavin' Blindburn though we both be born 'ere," Mrs. Wilkes added. "There be too much pain for us." She pressed her hand on her stomach. "And wi' another on the way, we wanted to get out a'fore it were born."

"Do you remember what the weather was like that day?" Agrippina asked.

The both of them exchanged glances as they tried to remember.

"It were a nice warm day in the beginning, but i' stormed after," Mrs. Wilkes replied.

Her husband nodded. "Aye, it did. I remember we thought

she were late 'cause she were waitin' out the storm wi' Mrs. Thrasher."

"Yet, she never made it." Agrippina blinked as she absorbed the information.

"Aye, though the storm began 'round the time we thought 'er to be there," Mr. Wilkes pointed out. "Or were hopin' she were."

Agrippina nodded, her brows furrowed pensively. "Would you be able to tell us which path she might have taken to get to Mrs. Thrasher's?"

"I do belie'e one of the Butler childers did see 'er walkin' toward thee hills," Mrs. Wilkes replied.

Mr. Wilkes nodded and pointed out a front window. "Aye, they say she most likely was headin' to a back way that cuts through some woods. Cuts the journey in 'alf." He described the beginning of the path's location, the start of it just visible from their front step. "The Thrasher farm be not three 'undred yards from the end o' the other side."

"And how long would it have taken her to get to Mrs. Thrasher's?" Agrippina noted the thickness of the woods, evident even from where she was standing.

"Oh, 'bout twen'y minutes or so." He nodded. "Though it would've taken 'bout for'y or more to go 'round the other way."

"Forgive me, but I have just a few more questions and they might be a little more difficult to hear," Agrippina began gently. "Where was your daughter found?"

The Wilkeses looked at the ground, both of them trying to compose themselves.

Finally, Mr. Wilkes cleared his throat to speak. "She were found several feet in the woods. Covered by some branches."

"Covered?"

They nodded.

"How long after she went missing was she found?"

"Four days," Mrs. Wilkes answered, looking down. "'Twere the storms that kept us from looking. We might've found 'er sooner if not for them."

"She 'ad only left the house not ten minutes a'fore she were killt," the father began to sob. "I were not far from her when it 'appened. I were home. I should 'ave gone wi' 'er. I could 'ave saved 'er."

His wife rubbed his back as he cried, comforting him in his grief.

"Thank you, Mr. and Mrs. Wilkes, for your time," she said. "We hope we can give you both clarity and peace of mind soon."

Mrs. Wilkes gave a somber smile and bowed her head. "I'm sure we'll ne'er 'ave either again, miss, but the thought is apprecia'ed."

The Greystones left, making their way back to the carriage, a little late for their appointment with Mr. Mackland though neither of them noticed.

"What are you thinking?" Dr. Greystone asked, speaking for the first time in a while.

Agrippina shook her head. "I noticed it this afternoon while I was going back through Dr. Johns's notes that Georgina Wilkes had an injury set apart from the other girls. She was attacked from behind. While the other girls were attacked from the front."

Dr. Greystone nodded as he listened.

"Now it is also apparent that she was attacked during the day. They said it rained after she left, but I have seen the way the storms here creep up on you. The sun very well still could have been out when she was attacked. Though, I imagine there is not much sun shining through the trees of those woods she walked through."

"I would imagine not," Dr. Greystone agreed.

"Why would the killer take the time to try and hide her body? None of the other bodies were covered up. They were left out in the open. Why would the killer do that?" she asked more to herself than her uncle. "Why would the killer risk being seen or heard by anyone?" She shook her head. "Unless—" She shook her head again, trying to gather the chain of events in her head. "She was the only one with any cuts to the back of her. The bite mark was not on her throat, but on her shoulder." She took in a deep inhale and let it out slowly.

"It does seem rather curious, does it not?" He offered her his hand to help her in the carriage when she paused.

Agrippina turned to the driver who was holding the door. "Sir, what does that patch of woods open into?"

The driver turned and looked for a moment and removed his hat before he spoke. "Well, miss, them woods lead to the valley. Ye can' tell from 'ere, but we're on a rise and them trees are on the top o' the south 'ill."

"Where Missy Hodgkin was found?"

He nodded as he thought. "Aye, miss, I belie'e that to be right."

Agrippina stared off at the woods for another moment before her uncle gently urged her in the carriage.

"Come, Aggy dear," he said looking at his pocket watch. "We are already late."

She absent-mindedly nodded as she obeyed, her mind too clouded with thoughts to be on anything else.

12

THEY ARRIVED AT MACKLAND MANOR JUST AS THE SKY turned a little grayer, threatening to rain, and were greeted by Rebecca Carne. The maid flashed her almost toothless smile as she let them in.

"Miss, good tuh see ye again," she said in admiration, ushering them into the parlor.

"Miss Carne," Agrippina replied with a slight nod of the head. "This is my uncle."

Her uncle also nodded in greeting.

"I'll tell the master ye arrived." She gave an awkward curtsey and turned to walk away.

"Your limp, Miss Carne," Agrippina began, causing the young woman to look at her. "It appears to be better."

Rebecca appeared abashed and uncertain of what to say.

"Do you still have the salve Francine Mellows had made for you?"

A strange emotion flashed through Rebecca's eyes, and she looked away for a moment. "Aye, it helped. Though me limp is always worse with bad weather. I always know if it'll rain 'cause me leg becomes more stiff." She bowed her head.

"I'ma get the master now and let him know you be here."

"This house is not what I thought it would look like on the inside," her uncle commented once Rebecca had left, staring at the décor.

"The dead animals do make it seem a little bleak, but it is not as dark as you thought it would be, is it?"

He nodded.

Mr. Mackland soon entered, smiling. "I am glad you have come."

"I am sorry we are a little late," Dr. Greystone told him, bowing. "We thought we should talk to a few more people before we settled down for the evening."

Mr. Mackland nodded. "Of course," he replied, unoffended. "You both have a job to do and do not seem like the type of people to do anything halfway. I think I would have been disappointed if you had not stopped to talk to anyone on your way here."

"That is kind of you to think so highly of us, sir." Dr. Greystone looked around the room, noticing the wolf in the corner. "I was just admiring your decoration."

Mr. Mackland chuckled. "A little depressing, I know." He sighed. "But every Mackland for generations has added to this collection. Except for myself, really. I was shipped off before the interest to hunt ever really sunk in. My father wanted me to have a better education instead of wasting my time chasing after poor animals, I suppose."

"Yes, Aggy told me you are a bit of a world traveler."

Mr. Mackland glanced over at Agrippina who returned his gaze, but only for a moment. "I suppose I am. Or, was, at least. My father sent me away when I was fifteen to London for three years, then two years in France and Spain, and one in Germany, and Italy. I had finally made it to Greece when my father passed away. I think I was only there for six months."

"That would account for your terrible Greek," Agrippina commented.

He smiled. "Yes, I believe that does."

Dinner was soon announced and the three of them made their way to the dining room, their footsteps echoing through the large room.

"Might I ask for what purpose your father sent you so far for your education?" Dr. Greystone asked as they sat down to eat, his curiosity getting the better of him. "Was he not satisfied with the British schooling? Being a Cambridge man myself, perhaps I am biased, but surely sending you there would have done you well."

He nodded. "I do not disagree. My father, however, never liked it here and wished he could have traveled, but his father never allowed it. Blindburn has been home to the Macklands for several generations and my grandfather was proud of that." He sighed. "So, my father sent me away in order to live out his wish of travel through me and broaden my horizons beyond our little town."

There was a brief pause as plates were set out in front of everyone, the sound of china clinking against the wooden table the only noise.

"Over nine years away from your home must have been difficult," Agrippina surmised, sipping her soup. "Moving to a new place so often as that? Having to get accustomed to the different cultures, languages, and religions."

"It was not so terrible," he replied. "The religion part was probably the easiest to overcome, if you can believe it."

She lifted a thoughtful brow. "Are you a papist, then?"

"Would that bother you if I were?" Mr. Mackland had asked her so softly and filled with emotion it made the question sound more like a plea.

Agrippina blushed and quickly shook her head. "I do not hold a prejudice against someone over the semantics of religion. Whether Catholic or Protestant, in the end, we are praying to the same God."

He smiled at her again. "Some would call that statement heresy, as reasonable as it might sound, but I agree."

Dr. Greystone, for a moment, almost felt like he was intruding if his host had not returned his attention back in his direction.

"I had a letter from a Thomas Beresford today," he said. "He informed me of some of your many adventures with your late brother."

Agrippina started. "What would Thomas write to you for?"

"To commend the two of you, though I see neither of you need help in that regard." He took a sip of wine. "He spoke very highly of the both of you." He rested his eyes on Agrippina who seemed unfazed by the comment.

"We have known each other since we were children. My uncle tutored us at the same time."

"Without saying my niece is wrong, she, more or less, forced herself into Lord Thomas's lessons. She would not take no for an answer." He chuckled. "She was as determined a child as she is a woman."

"I am sure of it." Mr. Mackland smiled again.

Agrippina looked less amused than the men did.

"But, I must say, I very easily relented. She was too bright to deny her knowledge," Dr. Greystone said affectionately. "I will always refer to her as my best student."

Agrippina shifted uncomfortably in her seat, disliking being the center of attention. "Yes, well, you cannot give me all the credit, uncle. You made learning easy," she stated, trying to put the subject about her to rest.

"How strangely modest of you," her uncle replied skeptically.

She ignored his remark.

"What is your opinion on the werewolf theory, Mr. Mackland?" Dr. Greystone asked as the next course was served.

Mr. Mackland chuckled. "It is strange to think people still believe in such things as lycanthropy. I, for one, am not one of them. Nor do I take much heed about witches either. It was a sad business what the people did to Miss Bertie."

"Yes, it was," Agrippina said looking up. "Could you not have done anything to prevent it? You are a landowner. Are you not a magistrate?"

He shook his head. "No, I was asked to fill in when my father passed away, but I refused. I wanted nothing of politics. Though, I never regretted not taking the position until the incident with Bertie. As I had no authority, there was not much I could do but to protest. However, I did write to the man who was to be the judge and inform him of the mistake."

"You vouched for her then?" Agrippina said.

Mr. Mackland nodded. "Yes, I did. Though I suppose threatening the vicar with treason helped more than anything." He smirked. "Whose idea was that?"

Dr. Greystone laughed through his nose.

"That was my uncle."

"Indeed! Agrippina is not one for stretching the truth, I am afraid. She is too honest to be of use in times of need." Her uncle laughed again.

"You might be amused at my inability to lie, uncle, but I am sure some might find it a noble quality."

"Oh, I am not belittling your honesty, my dear. It is a respectful quality you have, but, to an extent. Some might wish that you are not all together so—" he paused, looking for the word.

"Forthcoming?" she suggested.

"—blunt," he concluded.

Mr. Mackland seemed entertained by the playfulness of Dr. Greystone's manner toward his ever-serious niece. He glanced from one to the other listening as they almost bickered in a loving manner. His gaze, however, always lingered a little longer on Agrippina.

"Uncle, that is enough teasing," she lightly scolded. "I know it is your favorite subject, but you know I always rise to it."

"Teasing you is not my favorite subject, my dear, you are," her uncle corrected. "I have never been prouder of anyone in my life."

"You are lucky to have such a kind uncle," Mr. Mackland said. "I only remember one of mine and he was never this friendly toward me or anyone really."

"Thank you, sir," Dr. Greystone began, "but I have been the lucky one. There is no one more thoughtful than my niece, though she may not show her affections, she is always thinking of me in some way or another."

"Your maid told me something very strange after I was leaving yesterday," Agrippina stated, changing the subject after a brief pause.

"How so?"

"She told me about some feud between this town and one just over the border in Scotland. She said we might want to look there thinking they might have cursed Blindburn. I was hoping to gauge your thoughts on the subject."

Mr. Mackland chuckled. "Ah, I was wondering when that was going to come up. Though I did not think my maid would be the one to do so."

"A feud?" Dr. Greystone repeated.

Mr. Mackland nodded. "There is a neighboring town over the Scottish border that Blindburn has some unresolved issues with and vice versa since before my grandfather was born. It has been going on so long no one really knows who is at fault anymore though each side lays blame on the other."

"What is the feud about?" Agrippina asked.

Mr. Mackland took a deep breath as he thought and let it out slowly. "To be honest, it begins how most feuds of this kind do. With a woman." He ventured a smile at Agrippina who felt herself blush.

"Ah, a failed love story then?" Dr. Greystone guessed.

Mr. Mackland gave a small nod. "To a degree." He paused to take a sip of his wine. "A Scottish woman—forgive me if I do not recall names, as I said the feud is very old—came to Blindburn looking for work and she found it on one of the farms. By all accounts, she was a hard worker, but not long after she arrived the cattle of a rival farmer began to die, and her farmer's wealth grew. Sometime after that, her farmer's wife became very ill and passed away, leaving him a wealthy widower with several children to care for.

"The woman, of course, stepped in and helped the farmer with his household. Raising the children, cooking the meals, straightening the house and the like. Then one day, they surprised everybody by announcing their marriage. The town was suspicious since she was a nobody, and he was a prestigious landowner.

"But then, one by one, starting with the males, the farmer's children with his first wife died mysteriously until it was only the farmer and his new wife. But pretty soon, even that did not last, and the farmer soon died himself, leaving everything to his widow.

"The town grew angry, believing her to be a witch. So,

they arrested her, tried her, and burned her without knowing that her father was somewhat a man of influence in the town of Upper Hindhope just over the border. He raised a mob and attacked some of the people of Blindburn, killing several. And ever since, we have hated one another. People from Blindburn are murderers and women from Upper Hindhope are all witches worth burning." Mr. Mackland let out a sigh. "I know it sounds ridiculous."

Agrippina nodded. "Well, I would not call her a witch, but it is almost quite certain she poisoned them all," she pointed out.

Mr. Mackand looked rather surprised.

"She whittled her way into the farmer's good graces. First, she kills the cows of a rival farmer, the she kills the wife. After that, she begins to care for his children probably like they are her own, making him believe that he cannot raise them without her, so he marries her. Then, for legal purposes, she has to kill the children of the farmer off first, because then they will not be able to inherit the farm if they are dead. Once she is guaranteed to be the sole owner, she kills the farmer." Agrippina shook her head. "She was not a witch, just a common murderess."

Mr. Mackland blinked at her for a moment, looking from her to her uncle and then back. "I have grown up on that story. I must have heard my grandfather tell me a hundred times before I was the age of ten, and never once since then did I ever think what you just explained."

"Sometimes it takes an outsider's eye to see something you are too close to see," Dr. Greystone explained. "It is a very good explanation, Aggy dear."

"Thank you, uncle. It reminded me of that recent case in London," she said. "The young woman who was a housemaid for the printer. She kept poisoning him to make him sick so she could nurse him back to health, and eventually he fell in love with her and married her. That in itself was considered scandalous, but then his sister found the arsenic she had been feeding him and she was charged with attempted murder."

"Oh, yes, I vaguely remember Mr. Fallow telling us a story such as that," Dr. Greystone nodded.

Agrippina furrowed her brow in thought. "Is Bertie from Upper Hindhope? I know she told us she is from Scotland, but if she is from that town, there is no wonder she has such a prejudice against her."

Mr. Mackland nodded. "I am not sure anyone, including Bertie, knows where she is from."

They all chuckle.

"Do you think the feud is something to consider?" Mr. Mackland asked.

Dr. Greystone thought a moment. "How far is this town from Blindburn?"

"A little more than five miles as the crow flies, but because of the terrain you are not able to travel in a straight line so, it is more like twenty some miles."

"Twenty miles?" Agrippina repeated. "I can hardly believe someone would travel twenty miles on horseback—for a carriage would be too noticeable—just to kill one woman and then return."

Dr. Greystone nodded in agreement. "And if they were to stay in town, someone would be bound to notice, as strangers seem to be met with some suspicion here."

Mr. Mackland nodded as well. "Yes, most of the town knows everyone, so they would notice if someone was out of place."

Agrippina shook her head. "Not to mention, we have come to believe one murder happened during the day."

The sound of shattering glass interrupted them, as Rebecca Carne fumbled with an empty plate, dropping it on the floor. Everyone turned in surprise to look at her, causing her to blush.

"Mr. Mackland, sir," she said breathlessly, anxiously. "I be so sorry. I'd not mean to—"

"It is all right, Becky," he told her gently. "It is just a plate. Are you all right?"

She nodded. "Aye, sir. It just slipped from me hand, it did." Her anxiety at having broken one of the china plates did not abate and she stood there unsure of what to do.

"Have Michelle help you clean it up," Mr. Mackland ordered softly. "There is no need to worry, Becky. Seriously, it is just a silly plate."

Rebecca nodded. "Thank ye, sir. Yer too kind." She bowed her way out of the room carrying the other dishes.

"Now, what were you saying about one murder happening during the day?" Mr. Mackland asked, bringing the conversation back around.

"Georgina Wilkes. She was walking from her house on the other side of the valley to Mrs. Thrasher's farm to drop off a scarf. Her parents expected her back in time for dinner but thought she had been delayed due to the rain." Agrippina nodded as she recalled her conversation with the Wilkeses. "Her mother even said the sun had been out when Georgina left, but she had never made it to Mrs. Thrashers as she was still in possession of the scarf when her body was found."

Mr. Mackland nodded. "Interesting, but you are quite right. That would make it even more difficult for someone unknown to the town to be passing through unnoticed, but how were there no witnesses?"

"She walked through the woods and meant to travel through the valley via the south hill. To go around meant she would have doubled her trip."

"Certainly." Mr. Mackland's brows were creased, pensive. "That is rather bold, is it not? To attack someone in the middle of the day?"

Agrippina sighed. "I believe it very bold, but there was a considerable amount of cover due to the thickness of the woods, more so than the valley where Missy Hodgkin met her fate." She tapped on the table. "At any rate, this case has me asking more questions than answering them."

"And, yet, you do not seem concerned," Mr. Mackland pointed out, smirking.

"Oh, this is the state my niece always wishes to be in," Dr. Greystone chimed in. "She is forever looking for a mystery to solve, something challenging, of course, that keeps her guessing."

"Do you have any theories then?" Mr. Mackland asked.

"None I can share at the moment," Agrippina told him. "Forgive me, I do want to offend you, but there are some things I should not share. Some things that should be kept just between my uncle and myself until we have all the information we need. We cannot have our ideas leaked and cause another mob to run someone down as they almost did with poor Bertie."

"That is quite understood, though slightly disappointing." He raised his glass and sipped from it. "I have noticed, Miss Greystone, that you have not touched your wine. Is it not to your liking? I have others."

"Oh, no, please do not trouble yourself, sir," she replied quickly. "I am not one for drink, therefore, your efforts would be very much wasted on me."

"You are a woman who knows who she is and what she wants. Nothing could ever be wasted on you."

The rest of the dinner went by pleasantly enough. Mr.

Mackland was as charming as he had been the day before when Agrippina had first met him. Her uncle was more than delighted with him and told her so on their way back to the inn.

"He is a very intelligent young man," he said as the carriage lurched forward from the drive. "And has lived a very interesting life for a man his age. He is—what—about five and twenty?"

"He seems to be around that age."

"Well, what is your opinion of him?" he urged. "He seemed very intrigued by anything you said, my dear."

"I think him very amiable."

"Is that all? Only amiable?" he lamented. "You are rather disappointing, are you not? You always wish to deny me any bit of gossip. Amiable." He scoffed. "Will you not even say handsome? Pleasing to the sight? Not unattractive?"

"Uncle, are we not here to solve murders?" She arched her brow at him. "If that is the case, then what does it matter whether or not I find Mr. Mackland attractive?"

"Because, my dear, I wish you to find joy in every situation and have the ability to find the silver lining when the sky is overcast."

She eyed him skeptically. "You have been acting rather strange lately. What is going on with you? You have never pressed the issue about me marrying or finding an attachment before, but now you seem to have made it your mission."

He creased his brow and shook his head. "No, no! It is nothing strange to wish my niece—whom I regard more like a daughter—to be happy and see her happily settled. Why should there be anything strange in that?"

Agrippina saw that he was upset and, not wishing to further injure him, agreed to placate him. "Understood, uncle," she said softly. "Mr. Mackland is not unattractive."

He laughed through his nose and nodded. "Yes, but I do think Lord Thomas to be slightly less unattractive, do you not?"

She thought for a moment before shaking her head. "No, I think Mr. Mackland superior in that regard."

Dr. Greystone nodded, happy to have opened his niece up despite the growing feeling of despair in the bottom of his stomach.

13

Agrippina Greystone was born the first and only child to the ninth Earl of Ipswich, Frederick Greystone and his wife Charlotte Greystone, nee Sanford. She was born on a snowy day in March 1771. The birth had been successful, and the mother and daughter were deemed out of danger by the attending physician.

Her father, who of course had hoped for a boy to inherit his title, melted at the sight of her. The disappointment he might have felt on hearing he was to have a girl quickly vanished as he held her. *A boy could never be so perfect*, he thought.

The new family was happy for the next two years, their love for one another only growing, as Agrippina, named for her father's love of everything Greek, developed into a beautiful little girl. She was bright, even then, easily learning her letters and numbers. She was considered too young to begin lessons, but her father had insisted on it. So, from a young age, Agrippina learned to enjoy learning. Her parents couldn't have been prouder or happier of their gifted child. But, like flowers blooming with the first thaw, it was not to last.

It began with a cough. Charlotte, who was rarely ever sick in her life, could not stop coughing. Incense was burned, teas were brewed, and several trips to the healing waters of Bath were made, but to no avail. Charlotte continued to cough. And then, one day, that cough produced blood.

Horror struck through their seemingly perfect life as they both knew what was to come. Agrippina, too young to understand the seriousness of the situation, was removed to her father's newly married brother's home in Cambridge while her father stayed behind.

Her mother did not suffer long after that, but her father, brokenhearted at the loss of his beautiful wife, did. It was months before Frederick Greystone could retrieve his child and months after that before he could look at her without tears in his eyes, for she looked so much like her mother it broke his heart all over again.

He did recover from his grief, however, and poured himself into the education of his daughter. He thought every tutor he hired inadequate, firing them, and resolved to teach her himself. For years it was just the two of them reading aloud to one another, rarely leaving their estate. It was not until the death of his younger brother's wife and infant child years later that they stirred from the grounds.

For the next year, it was the three of them. The widowers pouring into each other their grief, finding joy in the only light in their life, Agrippina. But even this situation could not last and like his wife before him, Frederick Greystone grew very ill. He died within the year leaving his seven-year-old daughter an orphan, and Alfred Greystone her sole guardian and next in line as the Earl of Ipswich.

Noble titles, however, were not for him as he much preferred the comfortable, humble life of an academic and

Professor. The title of the tenth Earl of Ipswich was, therefore, quickly passed to a younger half-brother barely in his twenties who greedily took up the opportunity. To protect Agrippina's interests, however, it was agreed that this half uncle would legally adopt her, guaranteeing her an inheritance of forty thousand pounds. It was further agreed he would have nothing to do with her upbringing. Dr. Greystone was determined to raise her as his own.

Fifteen years passed and Dr. Greystone loved his niece more every day. He was proud of her accomplishments. Her desire to learn what she did not know; her ability to absorb information; her mutual repugnance to titles; and her immunity to the charms of men. For fifteen years, she had been his joy, his reason for living and carrying on as he did. If he had ever had a daughter of his own, he thoroughly believed he could never have been prouder of her than he was of Agrippina.

He was proud, yes, but concerned. Concerned for her future because very lately Dr. Greystone had begun to cough, and even more recently, that cough had produced blood.

Agrippina awoke in another panic. She sat up, gasping for air, unable to remember what it was she had dreamt about. She leaned against her headrest and took several deep, calming breaths.

Eyes. She remembered seeing eyes.

She shook off the feeling of unexplainable fear and made her way to the window. It was going to be another gray day. She continued to stare, watching as the working-class people below walked about the early-morning streets to wherever they worked. After a couple of minutes, she moved away from the window and began to dress, thoughts of the investigation running through her head.

She mainly pondered on why Georgina Wilkes had been attacked from behind. It bothered her, the difference between the cases. She was not sure why it bothered her, but she knew it might be important.

She sighed as she watched the dusk of the morning grow brighter and with her incessant thinking getting her nowhere, she finished dressing for the day and went downstairs. Her uncle had not yet risen and not wishing to inconvenience Mrs. Bragg, she decided she would go for a walk.

She made her way out into a subtle fog, the dirt damp with dew. She walked along the path passing a few of the shops just beginning to open and start their own routines. Some of the owners bowed their heads tentatively at her as she walked by, others merely stared at her.

She pretended not to see them as she went by as it was evident they did not want to force their civilities on her. When she reached the end of the lane, a turn in the road blocked by a quaint, little house, she was surprised to see Vicar Harmon and Mr. Mackland walking together.

The vicar himself seemed startled as well and bowed deeply. "Good morning, Lady Greystone, it is a pleasure to see you this morning."

Agrippina forced a small smile. "Vicar, good morning. You are well, I hope?"

"Very well, thank you. Very kind of you to ask."

"There have not been any more attacks, have there?" she asked noticing the inquiring look she was getting from Mr. Mackland.

The vicar shook his head. "No, Lady Greystone, I have had no reports."

"I am glad to hear it." She turned to Mr. Mackland and

nodded. "Good morning."

"Good morning," Mr. Mackland replied. He then turned to Vicar Harmon. "Forgive me, sir, but would you mind if we parted ways here? There are things I have to discuss with," he paused and regarded Agrippina for a moment, "Lady Greystone."

She looked away.

"Why, yes, of course, you do, sir," the vicar said with a bow. "I am sure there are questions you have about the investigation." He tipped his hat at them both and bid them good day, hurrying off the way Agrippina had come.

"Lady Greystone?" Mr. Mackland began. "Have I been demoting you? Are you a lady?"

Agrippina blushed slightly. "I suppose some would consider it an offense to be denied their birthright of title, but it has never been how I felt."

He gaped at her. "Then I should be calling you Lady Greystone!"

"You should not because I do not wish it," she ordered sternly. "Titles are too prestigiously pedantic for me."

He looked at her with a curious smile. "Lady Gr—Miss Greystone, you become more interesting every time we meet."

Agrippina blushed in surprise not expecting a compliment to her statement.

"So, you are a lord's daughter then?" he pressed playfully.

"I am. My father was an earl, but he died when I was seven."

"I am very sorry to hear that."

She nodded. "Forgive me, Mr. Mackland, but I must be keeping you from something. Where were you heading?"

"If you ever keep me from anything, I know I shall always be delightfully entertained." He grinned when she blushed again in confusion, seeing it as a little game to do so. "To be honest, I was on my way to the butcher."

"The butcher? Do you run your own errands?"

He laughed. "I suppose men of my station tend to send someone out for them, but I like to do things for myself as you seem to as well. It is something we have in common, I have noticed."

She nodded in acknowledgement.

He held out his arm. "Shall you walk with me?"

She hesitated a moment, before she slipped her arm through his, feeling a strange lightheadedness by being so close to him.

"Where were you walking to?"

She shook her head. "I hardly know," she replied. "I suppose I would have turned in a moment. I was just out getting air, trying to clear my head. I keep mulling the same questions over and over in my mind without an answer. It is quite maddening."

"Anything I can help you with?" he asked, gently prodding.

She shook her head. "No, I could not—should not really—be asking you for help in your own sister's murder investigation." She paused a moment to look at him. "We are, however, going to meet with her fiancé."

He nodded. "I was wondering when you would. It was Hawkins who first thought something was wrong. I believe he is the one who found the horse."

"I find it rather strange that all of the young women were all on the verge of getting married when they were killed," Agrippina mused.

"Is it so strange?" Mr. Mackland suggested. "They were all of marriable ages, were they not?"

Agrippina moved her head from side to side. "My uncle made the same comment, but, all things considered, I think

Missy Hodgkin was rather young. At fifteen she was still a child."

He nodded. "I believe marrying young has a lot to do with the state of mind of someone. Those that marry young tend to have a matureness of mind."

She shook her head. "I disagree. I think it shows an immaturity. To marry young is to demonstrate a lack of understanding of what marriage is."

Mr. Mackland chuckled. "And what is marriage, Miss Greystone?"

"For men, marriage is a means in which to ensure his lineage by securing a woman who is a vessel for such a feat. For a woman, marriage is merely being passed on from her father's property to her husband's. She has no more say in her life than she did before."

Mr. Mackland was unsure if he wanted to laugh or scoff. "I am astonished at your perception on an establishment we humans have been practicing for centuries. Nay! Millenniums. Do you so look down on the idea of it?"

"No, not all together. It can be a noble constitution between two people who love each other, but it should never be rushed into. What I abhor is using marriage as a means to gain another's property, or to get out of a terrible situation. Ignoble reasons to marry make me weary of it."

He smirked. "I am rather surprised you are not married then, Miss Greystone," Mr. Mackland said.

"Should you be?" she retorted. "I am more surprised by your impertinent statement than by my lack of a husband."

He blushed. "Forgive me, it was rather rude," he replied, his lips curling slightly into a smile. "I did not mean it in an offensive way, but more out of curiosity."

"I am not sure how that would make it better, but at any rate, I am not offended," she told him.

He let out a sigh of relief. "I am glad."

"There was a man who tried to make me his wife, but I refused his offer," she told him as matter-of-factly as if she had just remarked upon the weather. "On several occasions."

"Indeed!"

She gave a nod. "Do not feel sorry for him, however. He is a sad, drunken, old fool who most likely never remembers asking me and, therefore, continues to do so."

Mr. Mackland laughed.

She sighed. "Then, there was another younger man, but his advances were quickly denied."

He raised a brow at her. "You are quite popular then?"

"Oh, not in the sense you might think. I do not deny I am attractive physically, and intellectually I hold my own. But that is not what makes me 'popular' as you say."

"No?" he asked amused by her directness.

She shook her head. "No, that would be my very large fortune I am already in possession of. It makes all the young men fawn and drool quite pathetically."

He stifled a laugh. "You are an heiress then?" he inquired. "I believe that and your nobility surprises me the most about you."

"Does it?"

He nodded. "I have met my share of heiresses and ladies in my travels, and you are by far the most interesting and the least self-gratifying."

"I guess I have lived a little more plainly than a woman of my means normally would, but I was never for a life of grandeur. It bores me."

He laughed again.

"Well, it does. My father taught me to appreciate knowledge from a young age, and later, my uncle continued to encourage it. There was never time to fret over silly things such as silks, and lace, and the latest Paris fashions. What enrichment could such luxuries bring to my mind when they are only meant to enrich one's vanity and pride?"

He smiled, bowing his head. "I must admit, to have a wife who does not trifle with such things is rather tempting."

Her skin prickled in half embarrassment at the words and she was not sure whether she wished to rid herself of him or continue their walk. She did not have to decide herself, however, as they reached the butcher's shop.

"If I were not pressed for time, I would certainly walk you all the way to Mrs. Bragg's," he said in a way of apology.

She shook her head. "Please, do not let me hinder you in your errands. I am quite able to return on my own."

He stepped away and bowed gallantly. "It is always a pleasure, Miss Greystone." His eyes locked onto hers and she could feel her cheeks burning, unable to look away.

"Mr. Mackland." She finally curtseyed and hurried off, her heart pounding. After walking several yards, she ventured to look behind her astonished to see he was still standing in the street, watching her go.

14

Dr. Greystone stirred as the carriage pulled up to the ostentatious manor of Mr. Stanley Hawkins. Agrippina gazed upon it herself with a half scorn, already judging the inhabitants by the looks of the house they lived in.

The high windows, the marble fountain, the overdone hedges in the front screamed for attention, attention the inhabitants undoubtedly felt they were due. It made Agrippina want to laugh that a house this far out in the country, in the middle of nowhere—a place she had never known existed until a little over a fortnight ago—should try so hard to look so grand.

No, Mr. Mackland's house was sensible here. This was almost impertinent.

They were handed out of the carriage by overdressed servants and led inside to a grand hall, their footsteps reverberating off the marble floors. Agrippina tried to contain the scowl she knew she felt.

"New money," she whispered, "is always gawdy, trying to make up for the time their family had none to the point of shamelessness."

Her uncle lifted a questioning brow at her and opened his mouth to respond when a pretty young woman glided down the stairs in a satin dress, her hair done up in the current style. She smiled pleasantly, but Agrippina could tell she wished she was anywhere but there.

"Good morning to you," she said welcomingly. "I am Sally Hawkins. My father and brother are indisposed at the moment, but I can certainly help assist you." She ushered them down a long hallway past the walls cluttered with art and tapestries.

Agrippina wanted to groan at the ostentation of the scene, but refrained. She did, however, pause a moment when she spotted movement out of the corner of her eye as they passed an intersecting hallway. She took a step back, noticing two young men rolling a large barrel and slipping behind a tapestry. Her curiosity piqued, she turned to move down that hall when Sally Hawkins called back to her.

"This way, Miss Greystone!" she called gently.

Agrippina slipped away the memory of what she saw and followed the young woman who led them to a room in the back of the house that afforded a view of the River Coquet and ordered tea.

"Miss Hawkins," Dr. Greystone began, "we are here to discuss the day Miss Mackland went missing."

She paled a moment and nodded. "Poor Karen," she said softly. "She was a dear friend. I had never been more shocked in my life than on that day."

"You both were supposed to travel to Edinburgh, correct?" Agrippina asked looking around the more subtly decorated room.

She nodded. "Yes, we were to go shopping for her wedding clothes. Oh, poor Karen. Marvin—that is my brother—was bitterly upset. He loved her so very much. Since they were children, really."

"Were you one of the search party?" Dr. Greystone produced a small cough, stifling it with a handkerchief.

"Oh, heavens no! Father would never have heard of it." She shook her head. "No, Marvin, of course, rushed to find her, and father had some of the servants attend him, but—"

"All we found was her poor horse."

They turned to see a handsome, somber-looking man leaning across the doorway. He looked worn, as if he had recently lost weight he didn't mean to lose.

"Marvin," Sally said standing. "These are the Greystones. They are wishing to hear about—" she paused, looking uncertain, "Well, they are here about Karen."

He nodded. "Yes, I heard the rumors about them, whisperings from the workers. A man and a woman from London."

"Cambridge," Agrippina corrected. "London has its own murders to deal with, I am sure, being run amuck with newly immigrated Loyalists from the former colonies."

Marvin smirked, too fatigued to laugh, perhaps, and nodded. "Yes, indeed."

"Oh, Marvin, please sit," his sister begged. "I have ordered tea. It is so dreary out and you might catch a cold from a draft standing half out in the hall that way."

"I am fine, Sally," he replied, though he pushed off the doorframe and entered the room. "Now, how can I help you, Mr. and Mrs. Greystone?"

Agrippina cleared her throat. "Dr. and Miss, if you will."

"Forgive me. I should not have assumed."

Agrippina looked at her uncle who nodded in encouragement. "Mr. Hawkins, first allow me to say, I am very sorry for your loss. I have been told by several people of Blindburn what a wonderful and gentle woman Miss Mackland was."

He nodded, but didn't reply, unable to trust his voice.

"Our questions are not meant to cause pain, so, please, forgive us beforehand if we seem impertinent, but understand that every piece of information, no matter how small, might be important to help us solve this."

He didn't move for a moment, as if he were taking in everything that she said. Finally, he nodded. "I shall do what I can to help," he replied quietly.

"What first alarmed you to Miss Mackland's disappearance?" Agrippina began.

Marvin Hawkins took a deep breath and shook his head. "Karen was coming here because the next day she was to go shopping with my sister. She had said she would be here in time for an early supper, but supper was ready and she had yet to arrive." He shifted his gaze to the ground. "We waited another hour, but when she still had not come, I grew worried. She was a very good horsewoman, but her horse was new and not completely trained. I was nervous she could have been hurt, so I set out to look for her. I never could have imagined—" He paused and wiped his mouth.

"Please do not make him continue," Sally begged lightly. "It pains the both of us to hear it."

"Hush, Sally!" her brother scolded. "This has nothing to do with our feelings. If you do not wish to hear it, you can leave, but I want justice for Karen."

His sister looked ashamed that she spoke at all and resigned herself to sit and listen.

He cleared his throat as he regained his train of thought. "It had rained earlier that day, I believe, so the roads were slick, but I rushed with my horse to meet her. My father advised me to wait, thinking she was only delayed, but," he shook his head, "I could not." He stopped and looked at Agrippina with his dark, sad eyes. "It would not have signified whether I waited or left right then. She was nowhere to be found. There was only her horse with its leg broken."

Sally gasped and sniffed, standing and walking to the other side of the room.

"We searched for her, but it wasn't until those young boys found her that we knew what had happened to her." He took a long blink. "My poor Karen, whatever happened to her," he shook his head, "she did not deserve it. Nobody does."

"And poor Mr. Mackland having to identify her body," Sally lamented.

"Poor Mr. Mackland?" her brother repeated angrily. "There is nothing poor about that man."

Dr. Greystone and Agrippina exchanged small glances.

"I loved her," he said quietly, his gaze to the floor. "She was my moon on a starless night." He gave a shake of his head. "We did not care that my father and her brother disapproved the match. It was what we both wanted."

There was a brief pause.

"Forgive me. Did you say Mr. Mackland disapproved your engagement to his sister?" Dr. Greystone finally asked.

Marvin nodded. "My father did not care for it at first either. But he learned to accept it and even looked forward to it, though he saw it more as an advancement of our status. Our names joining with an ancient one." He shrugged. "That was not what we cared for."

"But why would Mr. Mackland disapprove of your engagement?" Agrippina pushed.

He shrugged again and shook his head. "I do not know," he sighed regrettably. "He did not shy away from his feelings though. He did not go so far as forbidding the match and seemed to understand it was what she desired. However, he was never friendly to me when I came around and if he ever met my father, well, their dislike is almost palpable."

"That is quite interesting," Dr. Greystone mumbled. "I

wonder what the issue could be."

"That is not information I should ever share with strangers."

Like his son before him, Mr. Hawkins approached the doorway without being noticed, leaning against the frame.

"Papa!" Sally exclaimed a little surprised. "Why, I did not expect you back today or else I would have made sure we had fish for supper!"

"That is quite all right, my dear. I came home a day earlier than I had said," he replied without taking his eyes off his guests.

They were hastily introduced by Sally, who, by that time, found nervous employment fixing tea for everyone.

"Huh," Mr. Hawkins uttered as he sat across from them. "So, these are the investigators?" He eyed Agrippina haughtily. "And what qualifications do you have?"

"I can assure you that I have more qualifications to investigate the murders of these young women, than you do to run your illegal distillery," Agrippina replied haughtily.

Sally looked perplexed; Marvin looked astonished; her uncle looked impressed; Mr. Hawkins smiled coyly.

"And I can assure you, I have not the slightest clue as to what you are speaking of," he said still smiling.

Agrippina motioned with her head to a table across the room with decanters on it. One was crystal, an amber liquid visible inside while another, smaller one, was an old foggy looking bottle. "That, I shall assume is from an older batch and that," she again indicated with her head to his shoes, "is corn dust. There are no mills in the area and I have already noticed that the farm animals eat hay, not corn, so it begs one to wonder, why should your shoes be covered in it? And then, there was that distinct smell of alcohol on you as you walked in. Not the same smell as if you have been drinking, but that sweet, sour smell of mash." She narrowed her eyes at him. "Did you spill some on you while sampling?"

Mr. Hawkins chuckled. "What interesting observations you make," he replied. "Though you have no proof to back any of that up."

She sighed. "You misunderstand my meaning, sir. We are not here for your silly distillery. We are here for the murders of five young women."

He shrugged. "They were nothing but animal attacks. What more could you investigate?"

"If that were the case, was a hunt organized to find the animal responsible?" Agrippina pressed. "Did anyone try to track the animal down and kill it?"

Mr. Hawkins did not reply.

"No," she replied for him. "Instead, the town's people arrested a poor old woman and accused her of witchcraft. Is that the kind of ridiculous stain you want left on your town's history or do you want to find justice for the young woman who was supposed to be your daughter-in-law?"

He gave her an amused look. "I do admire a feisty woman," he said looking at Dr. Greystone. "You never know what to expect with them."

"Father, please," Marvin whispered. "They are here to help Karen."

"Ah, yes, unfortunate event," Mr. Hawkins said unfeelingly. "It is a waste. She was a very pretty girl."

"She was an angel," Marvin breathed sadly.

Mr. Hawkins cleared his throat, seemingly ashamed of his son's emotional exhibition. "Well, at any rate, no one in this household had anything to do with the fate of Miss Karen Mackland."

Agrippina blinked at him. "We were not supposing that you did."

He met her gaze with a cold smirk. "Then you are done here?"

Dr. Greystone cleared his throat and stood. "Quite," he said with a nod. "Thank you all for your time." He bowed his goodbye, a gesture that forced Agrippina from her seat to do the same.

"I shall escort you out," Marvin said, rising from his seat.

"That is quite all right, sir. We remember the way. Good day to you all." Dr. Greystone turned and left the room with his niece in tow. "How in the world could you have guessed about the distillery?" he whispered in amazement when they reached the carriage.

She shrugged. "When we first arrived and Miss Hawkins ushered us down the hallway, I witnessed two young men disappear into the wall while rolling a large barrel."

"And what made you suppose it was filled with whiskey?"

"On first observation, I, of course, could not have made any guess as to what the barrel contained." She shook her head. "No, it was not until Mr. Hawkins came in smelling of sour mash that I made the conclusion." She huffed. "This is obviously how they have made their fortune or at least part of it. New money to be sure, but it does go to show, money cannot buy good breeding."

Her uncle laughed huffingly. "Aggy my dear, how snobbish you sound!"

"You will not shake me from my opinion. Mr. Hawkins is one of the most disagreeable men I have ever met with though our meeting was only a few minutes."

Dr. Greystone sighed. "I cannot disagree with you there," he told her. "Though the children certainly seemed better behaved than him."

She nodded. "I will agree with you on that. His poor children, to be fathered by such an unfeeling man."

"Do you think the distillery pertinent at all?"

She shook her head. "I am not sure. I think it could be purely coincidental." She frowned after a moment. "I do find it strange that Mr. Mackland did not mention his disapproval of his sister's engagement. We shall have to ask him about it."

Dr. Greystone nodded. "His manor is on the way; we can stop and inquire of it."

They did stop and within fifteen minutes of leaving the Hawkins', they were let into Mackland Manor by poor Rebecca who hobbled them into the parlor. Dr. Greystone sat down with a sigh, suddenly looking pale.

"Are you all right, Uncle?" Agrippina whispered in concern. "Perhaps you should move closer to the fire."

He shook his head and gave a wave of the hand. "I am fine, my dear," he replied with a smile. "I am a little tired is all."

Agrippina wanted to reply that he had been 'a little tired' for far too long and she was beginning to worry, but before the thought could be finished, Mr. Mackland walked into the room, a broad smile on his face.

"Good afternoon to you," he said after a deep bow. "Can I offer either of you anything?"

Agrippina shook head. "No, thank you. We will not take up too much of your time. We have just come from speaking with the Hawkins family and I have a follow up question for you."

He nodded slowly. "Of course."

"Were you against the engagement between your sister and Marvin Hawkins?" Agrippina asked without hesitation.

"Yes," Mr. Mackland replied just as quickly. "I opposed it. Greatly."

"Might I inquire as to why?"

He huffed. "I have no issue with the son, per se, but the

father is a scoundrel and it disgraced me to think that my blood would be connected to him in any way."

"There is no feud or hatred between you?"

"As a gentleman, I try to dissuade myself from hating anyone, but I find Mr. Hawkins deplorable and without honor."

"On a personal or business level?" she challenged.

He looked taken aback a moment. "I beg your pardon? I do not know what you mean."

Agrippina walked over to the small bar at the far end of the room and lifted up a bottle similar to the one at Mr. Hawkins's. "Did he cheat you out of the business? Refusing to give you your due after your father passed away?"

Mr. Mackland reddened, but only for an instant. "What are you supposing?"

"The distillery. Your family had a hand in it too, did they not?"

He shook his head. "I beg you, Miss Greystone, not to assume what you do not know. My negative feelings toward my sister's engagement had nothing to do with her untimely death and is, therefore, none of your business."

"Aggy," Dr. Greystone said softly.

She shook her head. "I thought for a moment it might not be, but now I have come up with a theory."

"Have you?" Mr. Mackland asked a little heated.

"Yes," she said just as defiantly.

"Pray, tell us what it is you think happened!" He threw his hands up as if saying "be my guest."

"Mr. Hawkins is an opportunistic man and he saw the engagement between your sister and his son as an opportunity of a lifetime."

"I cannot argue that point!"

"But you saw it as a slight, as an enemy taking control of something that is yours and therefore gaining ground on you. You could not bear the thought of it, so you devised a plan."

"Aggy," her uncle said in a sterner tone. "Do not say it."

"You wanted to hurt Mr. Hawkins's business, so you decided to strike at him, but you could not do it directly." She shook her head. "No, you had to strike at the people who help make his business possible."

"Enlighten me, please," Mr. Mackland urged, his anger not abating.

"Hannah Marks's father worked as some sort of guard for the distillery and the movements of products, but was fired not too long ago on the account of drunkenness; Francine Mellows's fiancé, Mr. Higgins was an out-of-town connection, the owner of the Dancing Bear pub in the next town over who drowned himself not long after her death; Missy Hodgkin's fiancé is the cooper's son and makes the barrels for the storing of the whiskey, but I could tell from the lack of sawdust and finished product in his shop that he had not been very productive recently; Georgina Wilkes, well, her parents both work at the distillery by the same dust on their shoes and smell of sour mash on their clothes and informed us they intend to leave town; and Karen, your sister, was about to marry the son of the man who ran the whole operation."

Mr. Mackland stared at her in astonishment, his mouth open until the realization of what she had said sunk in. "You believe me to have murdered all of these women?" he asked in angry surprise. "Including my sister? You are accusing me of the unnatural crime of murdering my own flesh and blood?"

Agrippina stood firm. "I have heard of cases where mothers have murdered their own children," she justified. "It is not so farfetched to me that you could be capable of murdering your own sister."

"How dare you!" he bellowed. "To compare me to monsters such as that; it is unfathomable!" Spit flew from his mouth as he spoke. "Karen was one of the only living relations I have left and you dare to think I would kill her all because I do not agree with her aligning herself with a family such as the Hawkinses? And, therefore, to further my revenge, sabotage their entire illicit business by murdering innocent young women?" He shook his head, fire burning in his eyes. "Not only is your theory outlandish, and highly improbable- as who could actually foresee half of the things you have just said- it is also offensive. I will not hear of it!"

"Hear of it, or not, that is my theory."

"Well, it is wrong. I daresay you have heard this before, Miss Greystone, but *you* are wrong!"

Agrippina frowned.

"I have shown you and your uncle kindness since you have come here and I am being repaid in unfounded accusations!" he continued, still steaming. "For a moment, I thought you and I shared—" he stopped himself and gruffly rubbed his mouth with his hand.

She blushed. "If you think your kindness could have shielded or blinded me from the truth, then you are mistaken," she told him. "I will not be shaken from my convictions based on shared glances and blushing smiles."

Mr. Mackland took in a shaky breath and shook his head. "How am I to even answer to this? The audacity! The presumption! You have no evidence other than conjecture!"

"I shall find it," she replied, standing straighter. "Whether to condemn you, or change my theory, I will find the evidence I need!"

Her uncle, who had borne all of this in silence, began to cough, lightly at first then violently. He quickly pulled out his handkerchief, continuing to cough, throwing his body into spasms.

For a moment, Mr. Mackland and Agrippina forgot their anger and turned to him in concern.

"I shall fetch some brandy for you, sir," Mr. Mackland said hurrying to his alcohol stand and pouring him a glass.

Agrippina rubbed her uncle's back, trying to soothe him as he pulled his handkerchief from his lips revealing it to be speckled with blood. She stepped back in shock and alarm, gasping. Dr. Greystone looked up at her in apology before quickly wiping away the remaining blood from his lip and slipping his handkerchief back in his pocket.

"Here, sir, please, take this," Mr. Mackland urged, proffering him a glass, ignorant as to what transpired between uncle and niece.

He took it with a nod, thanking him and taking a long sip.

Agrippina remained silent, her nerves shaken.

Mr. Mackland moved closer to her. "I will not be so ungracious as to throw you out," he began in a low tone, "but once your uncle has regained himself, I will politely ask that you quit my house."

She nodded in reply still not enough composed to speak.

Dr. Greystone cleared his throat after a minute. "Thank you, again, sir," he said, his voice hoarse from coughing. "I am much obliged. Brandy, I often say, it the cure to almost everything." He smiled, though weakly.

"Come, uncle," Agrippina said softly, helping him out of the chair. "I believe we must get you back to Mrs. Bragg's."

He nodded and allowed his niece to escort him outside. Mr. Mackland looked as though he was going to stay, but after a moment's hesitation, he followed them to the carriage to help Dr. Greystone in.

"Miss Greystone," he said in a soft, yet reserved voice as

she moved to enter after her uncle.

She paused, feeling the emotion behind the words, and turned.

"I beg you reconsider your theory," he pleadingly whispered. He shook his head. "I did not kill my sister, or any of these women."

She took a deep breath and let it out slowly, suddenly feeling rather tired. "I still have some investigating to do, Mr. Mackland, but I find it all strange that every one of the victims somehow has a connection with not only the Hawkinses, but you."

He looked shocked at this. "How do you mean? Please, tell me so that I might have a chance to defend myself. Certainly, you cannot object to that."

She thought it over for a moment before nodding. "I see no harm in telling you why I have come to my conclusions."

"Thank you," he said graciously. "After you have seen your uncle safely back to Mrs. Bragg's, then. I can meet you for a late tea or, you can come back here for dinner."

She shook her head. "Do not think me so foolish as to find myself alone with you, Mr. Mackland," she replied a little offended. "I have accused you of murder."

He looked offended himself. "Miss Greystone, I have no ill intentions- no intentions indeed other than to clear my name."

She remained unmoved.

He nodded after a moment. "Fine, we shall meet on mutual ground. At the Rose Bud, then. There shall be plenty of witnesses, I suppose."

She agreed and they fixed on a time later in the early evening.

"I will clear my name, Miss Greystone," he told her confidently as he handed her into the carriage. "You shall see,

that though some of the evidence points at me, I am a gentleman, not only in word, but in deed."

15

"You are angry," Dr. Greystone said, more as a statement than as a question.

Agrippina took her time with her answer as she helped her uncle up the stairs of the inn, their carriage ride having been completely silent. "I do not know what I am," she decided, her tone flat.

"You should be angry," her uncle continued. "I should have told you. I meant to tell you. Many times over these past two months."

Her breath caught in her throat. "Two months? You have been keeping this from me for two months?" She gave him a hurt look as she helped him into a chair.

Dr. Greystone looked ashamed. "Yes," he replied somberly. "It is something I am not proud to have kept from you, but you have known such hardship, such loss in your life, that I could not bear to—" He stopped himself and shook his head. "It does not signify. My reasons are not reason enough to have kept you in the dark of what you should have known."

"Uncle, we should not have left Cambridge, or at least,

we should not have come here! We should have gone else-where, like Bath or Lyme or perhaps the Alps. I have heard the mountain air is good for conditions of the lungs." She turned away as her emotions began to get the better of her, trying her best not to let him see her cry. "This, I imagine is the reason you have been pressing me to marry as of late? Because you fear there will be no one to care for me once you are dead?" She gasped and pressed her hand to her mouth and shook her head. "I should have seen this coming. You have been so tired recently, looking pale and coughing incessantly! I should have known! I should have known!"

"There, there, my child," her uncle said soothingly. "There is no reason to cry. I am not dead yet."

"Oh, uncle!" she exclaimed, hot tears rolling down her cheeks. "But you are dying!"

He nodded. "Yes," he said softly, "of that we can be sure."

"You should have told me!"

He gave another nod. "I know, but you cannot be angry. No, no, you cannot waste what time we have left being angry with me. There will be time for anger and sadness when I am gone."

His tone had been playful, but it did not have the effect on Agrippina that he had wished, and she burst into tears. The sight moved him as well as he had not seen her cry since the death of her father when she was seven years old. He held his hand out for her to take which she squeezed affectionately.

"I do not regret anything in my life," he told her. "More than most men, I am proud of the life I have lived; but more than anything, I am proud of you. You know that?"

She nodded silently.

"My choice to come here was partly selfish as I wanted to relive some of those glory days I shared with your father where we traveled England solving mysteries and crimes such as this." He paused to cough. "I wanted to share that with you."

Agrippina brought his hand to her lips and kissed it. "You have always done right by me, uncle. I could never have wished for a more wonderful guardian."

He smiled. "I am glad to hear it." He squeezed her hand for a moment before taking his back. "Now, enough of this melancholy business. We Greystones do not dwell on such distractions when there is business to be done."

"But, uncle—"

"I will not hear of it!" he proclaimed raising his hands. "We will talk of nothing but the investigation." He gave another cough. "We will talk of nothing but the investigation after you pour your poor uncle a glass of water."

Agrippina hurried to the water basin and did as he bade, waiting patiently for him to finish drinking.

"Ah, yes, thank you." He took another sip. "Now, where were we? Ah, yes, the investigation." He frowned. "I must confess, Aggy," he told her in a concerned tone, "the more I think of it, the less I like Mackland for these murders."

"Really?" she replied, a little astonished.

"I am not doubting your investigative skills or the strong connection between Mackland and the murders but something about it rings too easy," he explained. "Also, I am not sure why he, being the majority landowner and, therefore, due rent, would kill off some of his tenants or scare people from his land. A good portion of his fortune has to be from the those too scared to remain here."

"Is he the majority landowner?"

Dr. Greystone nodded. "I did some inquiring when you went to meet with him the other day. He owns the property where the families of those girls live."

Agrippina herself frowned as she considered what he was saying.

"He seems like a well-educated, reasonable man," Dr. Greystone pointed out. "Killing off a portion of his income does not seem a logical thing to do for a man that seems so logical himself."

She thought for a moment. "I see what you mean, though there is nothing *logical* I can see from these killings," she replied. "However, I was not overly convinced myself while I was explaining it. But something about the situation angered me and I could not stop myself." She sighed. "No, you are right, and I shall tell him so, but not until he has explained his connections to the murders to me. Though he may not be the murderer, I do think he has a connection to them. Whoever the murderer may be."

"Now, that I can agree to."

Agrippina looked ashamed.

"What is it, my dear?" Dr. Greystone gave another small cough and sipped from his water. "There is no harm in being wrong. We are all wrong at one point or another. If I had the strength, I would tell you all the errors I made during my time investigating the murder of that Baron's daughter. I must have accused more than three innocent people of the crime."

She shook her head. "Yes, but I showed a real unkindness toward Mr. Mackland. An unkindness he did not deserve."

Dr. Greystone regarded his niece for a moment. "What angered you so?"

Agrippina felt herself blush and moved to the window to hide it. "I do not know." She sighed. "He confuses me."

"You find him confusing? I do not know how. He seems to me a very straightforward kind of man."

She shook her head. "No, no, that is not what I mean." She

frowned. "I am confused by how, when he is around, I—"

There was a knock at the door interrupting them. Agrippina felt a little uneasy, but she moved to answer it.

"Beg yer pardon, miss, but there be a gentleman 'ere to see you," Mrs. Bragg told her.

Agrippina gave a surprised look. "Mr. Mackland?"

Mrs. Bragg smiled and blushed. "Oh, no, miss, 'tis not 'e. I'd 'ave said if 'twere. This be a man I've ne'er seen a'fore in my life. I did ask 'is name, but 'e said 'twould be more fun if 'twere a surprise." She looked amused.

"I shall be down directly. Thank you, Mrs. Bragg." Agrippina turned to her uncle. "I will be back shortly, uncle. You rest. I will have Mrs. Bragg bring tea up for you."

He gave an unconcerned wave of the hand in response, and Agrippina walked hesitantly down the stairs. She paused at the parlor door before walking confidently in. She was taken aback, however, when her visitor turned from the window to greet her.

"Thomas!" she exclaimed surprised.

He smiled and bowed gallantly. "Miss Greystone."

"What are you doing here?" she asked almost coldly, then immediately changing her tone said, "We were not expecting you. Your last letter gave no indication of your plans to join us."

He laughed. "I have caught the great Agrippina Greystone unawares, have I?" he triumphed. "I thought I might."

"I am not sure how 'great' I am," she replied with more modesty than she had ever shown before. "I do not know what I have done to deserve the title. Especially from a lord."

He laughed. "My word! I have never heard you speak so humbly. Where is your confidence? Usually when I praise you, you are the first to agree to it. You rarely have ever said 'thank you' for the compliments I have given you in years past."

His tone was playful, but she felt all the uncomfortableness of her character being under such observation.

"Have I been so ungrateful?" she asked almost sheepishly. "My uncle ingratiated me too much. I have grown up spoiled and arrogant. I apologize for my past behavior to you."

Lord Beresford looked astonished. "Dear Miss Greystone, I did not come all this way to plead for an apology. There is nothing in your character that begs for it."

Agrippina felt awkward and was unsure of where to look. "No, of course that is not why you have come." She forced a small smile. "To what do I owe the honor then?"

Lord Beresford stood straight as if standing in attention. "I have come to offer my services to you and Dr. Greystone." He furrowed his brows. "Where is your uncle?"

"He is resting upstairs."

"Ah, detective work is rather tiresome, I can imagine." He smiled. "Now, what conclusions have you come to? I half expected the case to be solved by the time I arrived, as brilliant as you are."

She shook her head. "Another compliment I do not deserve. I do not think I am even close to figuring this case out."

"What? I cannot believe that!"

She nodded. "It is true. There are so many working parts, but I am missing the one that connects them all."

"Come, come! Tell me everything. Perhaps a fresh pair of eyes and ears could help."

"Thomas, this is a very serious matter."

"Yes, and I am being serious," he assured her. "Do you not remember the two of us playing detective as children? Running around Cambridge finding the pieces to your uncle's puzzle that he would hide around the campus for us to find?"

She nodded with a half laugh. "Yes! How long ago that all seems."

"Well, I often think about those days, and they were by far some of the happiest of my life. Being under your uncle's tutelage and your scornful eye are times I look back upon with the greatest fondness."

She sighed. "Thomas, I cannot pretend to disagree to the fondness of those memories, but this is not a game. This is not the same as the scavenger hunts my uncle would set up for us. Five women have been killed."

He bowed his head slightly and nodded. "I know, and I can assure you that I completely understand that. I know my tone sounds jocular, but the gravity of the situation is not lost upon me."

She regarded him for a moment.

"Besides," he pulled a letter from his jacket pocket, "Lord Helston wrote me, asking me to oversee the whole operation. Though, I daresay I am a few days late." He handed her the letter.

Agrippina perused it.

"Seems Lord Helston went to school with a local gentleman, though the man seems to have passed some time ago."

She nodded. "Yes," she said handing the letter back. "The late Mr. Mackland passed away a little over a year ago, I believe. His daughter was the fifth victim."

He nodded. "Yes, yes, I remember from the letter. Have you been able to figure anything out?"

Agrippina blushed, remembering the afternoon's argument with Mr. Mackland and how unjustly she accused him. "I have theories, but as of right now, they are only assumptions and guesses, and we all know, Thomas, how I hate to make either of those."

He smiled broadly. "Indeed, I do. I have never met with a more serious person in my life than you, Miss Greystone. You were never one to judge without having all of the information."

She thanked him. "I do not oppose your staying and I am sure my uncle would love the extra company," she said, unable to think of anything else.

He gave another smile, an almost shy smile. "I was rather hoping *you* would enjoy my company as well."

Agrippina was at a loss for words and did not reply for several seconds. "Of course, I am always happy to see you, however, I am sure this visit will not have ample enough time for reminiscing and pleasure."

"No, no, it will be all business, I promise you. I did not come to get in the way of that."

She nodded. "Thank you. Then, perhaps, you would not be offended if I ask you to sit with my uncle this evening while I step out. I am meeting with Mr. Mackland to ask him a few more questions concerning his sister."

Concern flashed across his face. "Should your uncle not go with you?"

She shook her head. "My uncle has been suffering from headaches since this morning. Perhaps it is the higher elevation here." She forced a small smile. "Besides, this shall allow him the chance to fill you in on all we have learned so far. It shall be much more efficient this way."

He nodded slowly. "Of course," he replied readily, though with less vigor. Mrs. Bragg then came in with the tea tray and smiled at them. "I thought you might want a spot o' tea, miss. Your guest did come from so far and there is a chill in the air today. Though 'tis November, so a chill 'ere and there is to be expected."

"Thank you, Mrs. Bragg," Agrippina told her. "You are very

accommodating."

Mrs. Bragg looked pleased with the compliment and turned to exit the room when Bertie walked in, her face blank and her eyes in a dead stare. The innkeeper gave a scream of surprise at the sight of her and backed away.

"'Tis the devil ye'll meet wi' t'night. 'e be watchin' ye e'en when ye don' see 'im. But 'e always be there." Bertie swayed where she stood staring yet seeing nothing.

"Good God!" Lord Beresford exclaimed. "What on earth is wrong with her?"

"She is in a trance," Agrippina said rushing over to the old woman. "Bertie, can you hear me?"

"Be careful! Be careful! Thee devil sees ye. The devil be after ye!" Bertie prophesized. She then turned her dark eyes onto Agrippina and opened her mouth in a scream though no noise came out. She swayed once more before collapsing in Agrippina's arms.

Lord Beresford rushed over to help and picked the old woman up as if she were nothing, laying her gently on a nearby couch. "Smelling salts!" he ordered. "She needs smelling salts!"

But before anyone could move an inch, Bertie's eyes fluttered back to their normal hue of blue and she smiled. "Might I get a bit o' tea, ma'am?" she asked quietly as if nothing had happened.

Lord Beresford looked at Agrippina in bewilderment.

"I shall pour some for you, Bertie!" Agrippina told her, moving to the tea tray.

"'Tis not right, miss," Mrs. Bragg whispered to her. "There be somethin' not right 'bout 'er. She shouldn' be talkin' 'bout the devil like that. I thought she were to scare me half to death."

"Do not give into your fears, Mrs. Bragg," Agrippina

assured her. "She is old and prone to fits. I believe she is losing her mind, but there is nothing evil in it. She is merely verbalizing something that she has been taught to fear her entire life."

Mrs. Bragg shook her head. "I don' know, miss. Seems darker to me."

"Well, it might seem unsettling, but we must not let that interfere with our kindness toward her. She is a kind woman otherwise and deserves our charity."

The innkeeper nodded. "Aye, that be so. A very grateful woman to any kindness shown to 'er."

"We will not mention this to my uncle," Agrippina told her. "It might upset him, and he is feeling a little unwell."

"Oh, certainly we will not!" she readily agreed.

Agrippina thanked her. "Now, if you please, take this little cake to him and a cup of tea."

Mrs. Bragg curtseyed and hurried out the door.

"Miss Greystone, might you enlighten me as to what just transpired?" Lord Beresford said as she helped Bertie up and handed her the teacup.

"Nothing."

He looked at her surprised. "That was not 'nothing'."

"Bertie, how are you feeling? Better?" Agrippina asked the old woman, ignoring Lord Beresford's comment.

"Aye, miss, I thank ye," she replied, graciously sipping the tea. "Ye are thee most kindest soul I've met. Not since me own mother 'ave I've known such kindness, miss." She took Agrippina's hand and squeezed it. "Too good ye are."

Agrippina flashed a little smile and stood from the sofa. "Rest, Bertie, it will be good for you." She then motioned for Lord Beresford to follow her into the hall and gave him the account of Bertie and what she was to the case. She even told him of the other "episodes" she had had.

He looked at her with astonished concern, his eyes wide. "What are you to do?" he asked. "Surely, this case is more dangerous than you thought?"

Agrippina almost laughed. "What in the world are you talking about? She is just an old woman. There is nothing harmless in what she says. As I told Mrs. Bragg, she is old and is just losing her mind here and there. But she is harmless."

"Her statements do not seem harmless!" he exclaimed. "They seem prolific!"

Agrippina smirked, amused. "I am glad," she said in a light tone, "that you have not changed from the superstitious boy that you were of your youth."

He blushed. "I do not call it being superstitious, Miss Greystone, I call it being cautious, and I hope you take care."

She stood a little straighter. "I have always been cautious, you know that. Though we have not seen each other, say for the last meeting in Cambridge, in over five years, I am as cautious as ever."

He bowed his head. "I am relieved to hear it. I would very much hate for something to happen to you, Miss Greystone." His eyes slowly met hers and Agrippina felt the full force of what he had meant.

She cleared her throat and averted her eyes. "Now, I am sure you are tired, Thomas. Please, go and freshen up so that we might have some tea. It will be cold soon, I am sure, if you do not hurry."

He bowed and walked off, meeting her eyes for another moment before he sought out Mrs. Bragg for a room.

16

Agrippina snuck out of the inn earlier than she orig-inally planned, leaving behind her uncle in the care of Lord Beresford who came, no doubt, because he was bored with his life of luxury and indulgence, and felt he needed some excitement. Though, she could not help but think that he also came because of her. She saw it in his lingering looks and smiles.

He fancied her as her uncle thought he did before they left for this wretched place. Her uncle was always right about such things while she chose to remain blind to them until it was too late. That was how it was with that rich banker.

He had flirted and flitted about her, buying her small tokens of his affections, and she had written them off as kind gestures from one friend to another because that is what she chose to believe. She saw the impropriety of his attentions and, therefore, thought that he should have too.

Her uncle, however, warned her against accepting his gifts and smiles so easily. But, she had been young, and, though she was intelligent in the academic world, she was naïve in the real one and a girl of seventeen or eighteen cares only for what others might think of her. She had been appalled, however, when he proposed, rejecting him almost immediately.

Other than her lack of love for him, she was the daughter of an earl, and would never have thought to have stooped so low as to marry the son of a banker. She had seen through him the moment he brought marriage into the question. Despite his attentions, he only thought of enriching and aggrandizing himself.

That was not the case with Lord Thomas Beresford, the eldest son of a duke. At least, that is not what she thought as she made her way in the dusk to the Rose Bud. He had always been kind to her, but the difference was in his eyes. The way he looked at her was telling in itself and she almost imagined that Mr. Mackland looked at her with the same intensity.

She shook the thought away. No, that could not be true. She had only known Mr. Mackland a few days; she had known Thomas for most of her life. They grew up together, shared secrets together. Despite that, the lingering looks he bestowed on her only gave her the blush of guilt for not being able to return his feelings. The blushes that Mr. Mackland's looks invoked were—

She shook her head again. That was not why she was here. She was here to smooth out a mistake. To connect the dots left that needed connecting.

She stopped a moment in her walk to look up at the moon. It was full and she felt a wave of uneasiness despite herself. *The full moon. The time when the beast had the most strength*, she remembered from one of her uncle's stories.

There was a gust of cold wind rolling off the nearby hills and she shivered. The Rose Bud should be just around the corner. She picked up her pace, letting her irrational fear get the best of her and when she saw the glow of the pub dancing on the dirt street, she felt her uneasiness melt away.

She hesitated at the door, noticing the lack of horses tied to the post out front and thought she must have arrived well before Mr. Mackland. She glanced inside the window and hesitated more as she saw the large gathering of people drinking and eating.

How are we going to hear each other talk?

She moved to the door when movement caught her eye. She turned quickly to see what looked like a large dog ducking behind the building.

Probably a stray.

She took a deep breath, however, and pushed her way into the door, causing several in the crowd to stop in their conversation and notice her.

"Good e'nin', miss," Rebecca Carne said in greeting, giving an awkward curtsey.

Agrippina nodded to her. "Good evening, Miss Carne."

"The master should be comin' soon. 'e were jus' leavin' when I was."

"Did you walk all the way here from the manor?"

Rebecca shook her head. "Nay, I've my own li'l pony. Given tuh me by Mr. Mackland. 'e sees what a struggle it be for me to walk sometimes and took pity. 'e always do make sure I've not far to walk."

"That is very kind of him."

"Aye, 'e be the best man in Blindburn," Rebecca agreed. "'Tis a nice pony 'e gave too. 'Tis the brown and white one jus' out front. 'e's a bit scraggly to look at, but 'e's faster than he looks. 'is trottin' do get me where I need to go in no time."

Agrippina nodded. "Are you here alone?"

She shrugged. "Me cousin serves 'ere. She be keepin' me comp'ny when she can." She pointed to a young woman carrying a tray of growlers to a table. "And me brother'll be 'ere soon to walk me 'ome. Though 'e don' need to since I've Dusky. That's me pony."

"I am sure your brother just wants to make sure you are safe."

Rebecca nodded and smiled. "Oh, there be Master Mackland! What a sight! I 'twas surprised when 'e said 'e were comin' 'ere. 'e ne'er does." She gave another curtsey. "I'll see ye la'er, miss."

"Good night, Miss Carne." She turned to see Mr. Mackland hovering at the door, gazing at her.

He took his hat off and bowed when he was noticed, moving further in. "Shall we grab a table?" he asked using his hat to point to a set of vacant seats.

She followed him.

"I first want to apologize for my behavior earlier," he said as they sat. "I should not have lost my temper."

Agrippina was astonished and confused. Why should he think she was owed an apology? She shook her head. "There is nothing to forgive."

He looked at her in earnest and opened his mouth to speak, but not knowing what to say, he closed it again.

"Wha' can I get ya, lady and gent?" interrupted the barmaid.

Mr. Mackland hesitated. "Ale, please."

Agrippina for a moment was not going to order anything, but changed her mind before she spoke. "Might I have a whiskey, please?"

Mr. Mackland looked at her in surprise.

The barmaid nodded and swayed off.

"I did not think you drank."

"I do not always do so."

He nodded letting the air thicken in awkward

contemplation.

The barmaid soon returned, winking at Mr. Mackland as she placed the drinks on the table and went off again. Agrippina made the mistake of smelling her drink first and flinched. It was not a smell she was used to but sipped it anyways. It was strong and burned, but it instantly warmed her.

"I did not know about the distillery until my father died," Mr. Mackland began, taking his growler and staring down into it. "Even then, I did not discover it until I had been home for two months, going through the finances and seeing these strange earnings. When Mr. Hawkins approached me about it, I was ashamed at what my father had been doing. I admonished his dealings and said I wanted nothing to do with them. He laughed at me. Told me that what my father was receiving from his cut of the distillery was keeping the Mackland name afloat." He shook his head. "This made me angry, and I banished Mr. Hawkins from my house." He paused, looking a little embarrassed.

"That might explain your dislike of Mr. Hawkins, but it does not explain the connection between the victims and yourself or Mr. Hawkins," Agrippina replied gently.

He laughed through his nose and nodded. "That part is easier to explain. Half of the town works in some way or another for Mr. Hawkins. Even Mr. Thrasher did before he passed away. He rented out his mules for transport." He sighed. "There are not a lot of people living in Blindburn who don't have their hands in the distillery in one way or another." He finally took a sip of his ale. "If it were not for the distillery, as much as I would hate to say it, a lot of these folks would be without jobs." He shook his head. "I do not agree with the distillery's existence. It is the legality that bothers me, but I cannot discount how much the people of Blindburn depend on it for income."

"And the murders? How do you explain them starting only a few months after you returned?" she asked but without conviction.

He frowned and shook his head. "I cannot explain it," he replied. "Regrettably, that is a truth I cannot deny, but that does not make me the murderer. It is pure coincidence as far as I am concerned."

Agrippina felt ashamed at how quickly she came to her conclusion. She sighed. "I will not say that I have completely discounted you as a suspect for I have yet to count anyone out, but I will apologize for the way I spoke to you earlier. You deserved more than that."

He nodded. "Thank you." He lifted his growler in a 'cheers' motion before sipping.

Agrippina hesitated, but she lifted her glass in the same motion and took a sip.

"Might I be able to ask you a few questions?" he ventured.

She nodded, taking another slow sip.

"If you could be anywhere but here, where would you be?"

The absurdity of the question made her laugh, and she covered her mouth with her hand.

He smiled at her. "That is the first time I have heard you laugh," he pointed out.

She blushed and coughed in her confusion. "Your question caught me off guard is all."

"Well?"

"You were serious?"

He nodded. "Why should I not be?"

She thought for a moment and sighed. "I miss my estate at Ipswich," she confided. "Well, it is not my estate. It belongs to my uncle, Henry Greystone, the tenth Earl of Ipswich. Though I am sure it is nothing like I remember."

"Ah, the middle brother?"

She furrowed her brows and shook her head. "No, a half-brother, younger than my Uncle Alfred."

Mr. Mackland looked confused.

"Uncle Alfred did not want the title after my father passed, so Uncle Henry, the product of my grandfather's second marriage received it as long as he promised me my inheritance."

"Do you not see him often?"

She shook her head. "No, not at Ipswich. I have not been there since his wedding ten years ago. His wife disliked me, so even though he is my legal guardian, I am never invited to stay with them there."

There was shouting in the far corner of the pub and they both turned to see what the commotion was, but it was nothing one didn't expect from the local drinking hole. A drunk had merely fallen from his chair and his friends were laughing at him as he grumbled profanities. Agrippina saw Robert Carne scowling in the corner. He slowly made eye contact with her, the look in his eyes sending chills down her spine.

"Is that the only family you have?" Mr. Mackland asked, drawing her attention back to him.

"I have an aunt and uncle on my mother's side. I visit them once a year around Easter. They are only in London, so it is not too far." She regarded him for a moment. "Why are you so interested in my family?"

He shook his head. "Can I not be?"

"You have another sister, I heard?" she asked, done with talking about herself.

He nodded. "Yes, Mary. She is married and living in Derbyshire with her husband and five children, I believe." He looked pensive for a moment before nodding again.

"Yes, five."

She gave a small laugh. "You're not sure?"

"I have not met them, yet, but I hope to see them all for Christmas." He cleared his throat and looked away, his expression growing solemn.

She knew what he must have been thinking. He was thinking about his poor sister Karen and how last Christmas they were together and this Christmas they would not be. It is what she felt on her first Christmas without her father. She wanted to steer the conversation anywhere else, but she could not. However sorry she felt for his feelings, she had to think of solving the case.

"Were you personally against your sister marrying Marvin Hawkins or was it just the family connection?" she asked.

He looked confused at the change of subject, but shook his head. "No, personally, Marvin Hawkins is a good man from what I can tell and what I have heard. It is only the family connection I did not approve of."

She nodded. "He seems very different from his father. Both of the children do."

"Yes, they are not hardened as he is."

She looked pensive for a moment.

"What is it?"

She shook her head. "I am not sure," she replied quietly. "There is something about this case I am missing and until I figure it out, I will not be able to solve it."

"Are you against the idea that is was just a beast?" he asked.

She nodded. "Yes, I am. For several reasons, though I cannot share them with you."

He looked a little offended. "Why should you not be able to share them with me? I am a gentleman, an educated gentleman. Might I also not be able to give some insight being a local? There could be something I am not aware I know until you tell me."

"Mr. Mackland, you being a gentleman and a local has nothing to do with anything," she told him. "I cannot tell you because—" She stopped herself, unsure of what to say.

"Because you do not trust me?" he concluded with a nod.

"Trust has nothing to do with the issue at hand," she tried to explain. "There are some things only the murderer knows and if it gets out that I know them too, he could panic or change something or-" She shook her head.

Mr. Mackland stood. "I was a fool to think I could change your mind about me. I should not have wasted your time." He took a few coins from his pocket and placed them on the table. "Have a good rest of your evening." He placed his hat on his head a little angrily and walked away.

"Mr. Mackland!" Agrippina said standing, feeling a sudden wave of dizziness come over her. She closed her eyes for a minute, the intense sounds of the pub rushing over her, and the heat from the fire was suddenly unbearable. She staggered her way out into the moonlit, crisp night, bracing herself on the wall of the small building for momentary support. From the small cloud of dust in front of her, she could tell Mr. Mackland was already long gone.

She looked out along the dirt road, watching as it stretched out into the valley between hills and shook her head as she tried to focus her eyes. It was no use, however, and after taking a deep breath, she pushed off the wall of the Rose Bud and followed the road, walking unsteadily.

Her head began to pound, and she pressed her hand to her temple as she walked—stumbled—along the road. She breathed heavily, feeling the overbearing weight of her chest concaving into itself and for a moment she had to stop and regain her bearings. She looked around her, unsure if she was even going the right way, until she spotted in the distance the forest line. She nodded to herself and pressed on, her feet dragging heavily as she walked.

She shook her head again, confused as to why she could barely function. She could not be drunk. That could not be it. She did not even finish her one drink. Surely the few sips she did take could not have this effect on her.

Suddenly, the sound of running feet overcame her and she turned quickly to see a shadow dash by. She gasped, unable to see clearly in the dark and haze of her condition. She turned in a circle, searching for what the shadow could have been, but this only made her dizzier. Her breaths came in shakily as she pulled out the knife her uncle had given her. She gripped the handle tightly, unsure of her capability to wield it as the shadow dashed by her again, this time growling.

"Oh, dear Lord," she thought, or did she say it out loud? "It is a beast."

The growling was behind her again and she turned, her knife out in front of her, but it was too late; the beast had already lunged. Agrippina felt herself scream as she held her arm out in defense, the beast's teeth clamping down on her. She could feel the searing pain as its teeth sunk into her flesh. There was a brief struggle as she fell to the ground, the beast still clamped onto her forearm, when she remembered her knife.

Blindly, she jabbed the blade into the beast's side, causing it to cry out and release her arm. Agrippina sighed in relief, but the shock of it all fell on her and she slowly began to lose consciousness. That was when she heard it, a voice, a human voice.

She tried to figure out in what direction it was coming from, but her body was so heavy, she couldn't lift her head.

She heard the crunching of boots and a curious raking sound coming closer to her, but nothing more as the world faded into the darkness of the night.

17

AGRIPPINA WOKE WITH A START AND IMMEDIATELY REGRET-ted it. She gasped as her head pounded and she pressed her hand to her forehead to try and relieve some pressure. That did not help the pain in her forearm that soon began to burn and sting. She groaned when she saw the bandage, the memory, hazy as it was, of what happened coming back to her.

Once the fog of her brain lifted, she began to realize she had no idea where she was. The bedroom was not the one she had at the inn and the confusion of the situation caused her to panic. She threw the covers off and walked to the window, opening the curtains to let in the morning sun.

She squinted at the brightness, unused to the sun since they arrived in the grayness of Blindburn. She noticed from the view, however, where she was. She was at Mackland's estate.

"Yer awake, miss!"

Agrippina turned quickly, surprised by whoever spoke and immediately regretted it. She groaned as she pressed her hand to her forehead, the sharp pain nauseating.

Rebecca Carne hobbled over to her and gently took her under the arm. "Come, miss," she said softly. "Let's put ye back to bed. I'll go and get my master."

"What am I doing here?" she asked, gasping in pain as she lowered herself back to the bed, her body sore and bruised.

"Agrippina!" her uncle's voice came from the doorway. He rushed over to her.

"Uncle?"

He knelt by the bed, took her hand and kissed it. "My dear, you gave us all a fright!"

Rebecca moved to the corner of the room and sat in a chair to wait until she was needed.

"What happened?" Dr. Greystone asked, placing a hand on her cheek.

She shook her head. "I—I do not know," she stammered breathlessly, trying to remember. "I was attacked by—by some animal." She looked at the bandage on her forearm for a moment before she began to unwrap it.

"What are you doing?"

Agrippina ignored her uncle as she continued to throw the bandages off. She had to see it. She had to see if it had been real. She gasped when she had finished unravelling the cloth and gazed upon the unmistakable bite mark.

"What am I doing here?" she almost whispered.

"I found you," Mr. Mackland replied.

She jumped, unaware that he had entered the room.

"I felt uneasy about the way our last conversation had ended," he explained. "So, I came back to talk to you again and," he paused letting out a heavy sigh, "I saw you lying on the ground, lifeless. I thought you were dead."

Agrippina felt her heartbeat quicken and her skin prickle as she held her uncle's hand tighter. "You found me?" she asked, uneasy by the vagueness of his explanation.

He nodded.

"Is that all you found?"

He looked confused. "I do not understand your question."

"You saw nothing else? Just my body lying on the ground?"

"There was blood," he replied shaking his head. "I—I do not—there was nothing more I could see with as dark as it was."

Agrippina shifted her gaze to the side remembering. *Blood.* Her eyes grew wide as she realized she had stabbed the animal or whatever had attacked her.

"I injured it," she said breathlessly.

"What is that, my dear?" her uncle asked.

"The knife you gave me, uncle. I stabbed the creature with it!" she whispered excitedly.

"Do you think you killed it?" he whispered back.

She squeezed his hand to shush him. "Later," she replied as Dr. Johns walked into the room.

"And how is our patient?" he asked a little indifferently.

"You called a doctor?" she accused.

"What else could I have done?" Mr. Mackland asked. "I thought you would die otherwise."

"Yes, yes, call the doctor. No matter if he is sleeping in his bed. A frantic knocking in the middle of the night is sure to not give him an apoplexy at his age," he grumbled. He took her face in his hands and examined her eyes, tilting her head one way and then the other. "You seem to have recovered quite well from your hysteria."

Agrippina pulled back. "Hysteria?" she hissed. "I was attacked!"

He nodded begrudgingly taking her unwrapped forearm again. "Yes, yes, the bite wound is nothing, but the fear of it all caused you to collapse." He pulled out more bandages and began to rewrap it.

She shook her head, wincing at the pain. "No," she said with conviction, turning to Dr. Greystone. "Uncle, I believe I was drugged."

"Drugged? Good God!" Dr. Greystone proclaimed.

Dr. Johns huffed.

"Drugged?" Mr. Mackland repeated, taking a step closer. "How do you mean?"

She shook her head again, though slowly, in protest to his question. "I must get back to my notes."

"Aggy dearest, your notes can wait," her uncle replied.

"I wish to leave," Agrippina demanded a little more forcefully, pushing her way back out of bed.

"No, Aggy my dear, you must rest!" he urged.

"I can rest back at the inn." She moved toward her boots and sat on the large windowsill as she pulled them on, fighting the nausea rising in her.

"Miss Greystone, please, you should not be moved," Mr. Mackland tried persuading her. "Dr. Johns, tell her she should not be moved."

Dr. Johns opened his mouth to speak, but Agrippina cut him off.

"What should he have to say to change my mind?" she asked tying her laces. "He said himself just a few moments ago I am recovered." She stood and took a small moment to inhale as she made her way out of the room, her uncle and Mr. Mackland both making fusses behind her, disturbing Hubert and Angeline who had been curled up at the base of the stairs waiting for their master. They both lifted their heads up as she passed and once they realized she wasn't going to pet them, they laid their heads back down and resumed their naps.

Agrippina was determined to get out of the house. She was determined to get back to her notes and away from the confusion clouding her mind. She needed time to think and piece together what happened the night before.

"You could at least take breakfast before you go," Mr. Mackland told her. "It would make me feel more comfortable."

She gave another small shake of the head. "I thank you, but I am resolved to leave now."

"But I have not yet had a carriage prepared," he argued.

"Then I shall walk." She made her way to the door and was caught by a dizzy spell when her uncle thankfully took her under the arm.

"We shall sit and wait for the carriage, Agrippina," he told her in a stern voice.

Agrippina turned to her uncle, wanting to protest, but upon seeing the look on his face nodded and acquiesced. And thus, she was forced to breakfast; she was forced to sit and hold in her thoughts and feelings. The awkwardness of it all was almost unbearable as she avoided the eye of Mr. Mackland who seemingly tried to get her attention the entire time.

When the carriage was ready, Agrippina could not wait to get to it almost forgetting the fake niceties she had to bestow on her host. She curtsied and thanked him and was out the door before the uncle could tell her otherwise.

She did not seem to breathe until the carriage pulled away.

"Now," her uncle began after a minute or two, "what is so pressing that you thought you could border on rude to Mr. Mackland?"

"I've not the mind for civilities," she explained with urgency. "Uncle, last night, I did not pass out because of fear or hysterics! I was drugged. Last night, I was in the presence of the murderer."

He nodded, frowning. "Yes, you mentioned you were

drugged earlier and I have been dying for an explanation since."

"I could not give one earlier in that present company. I had to get away." She pressed her hand to her forehead and sighed. "I had ordered a glass of whiskey last night."

"Did you?" he asked, a little confused. "That is unusual for you."

She shook her head. "That is not the point, uncle!" she proclaimed. "The point is, I only had maybe two sips from my drink, yet, when I stood, I felt dizzy and my vison blurred."

"Why would you not stay at the Rose Bud and have a message sent for me?" he asked a little angrily.

"I could barely think!" she told him. "I was confused; my body was heavy; and I was tired. I had never been so tired."

She stared at the floor of the carriage as she remembered the night before. The moonlight dimly shining, the cold air on her face, the sound of the beast running toward her, the feel if its teeth piercing her flesh, the feel of the knife jabbing into *its* flesh, and the footsteps, that voice.

She abruptly looked up. "Uncle," she breathed.

He smiled, knowingly. "You have been bitten by the beast yourself. Are you becoming convinced as the locals are that we might have a demonic beast on our hands?" he teased.

Aggy shook her head. "Absolutely not," she stated confidently. "I am convinced more than ever we are still looking for a human."

"A human with very sharp teeth, eh?" her uncle chuckled.

"No, the bite wound is most likely from an animal. That I believe it is, but it is the only wound caused by one. Though I am not sure I would not call the man capable of such despicableness an animal."

Dr. Greystone gave a pensive nod, urging his niece to continue. "What is your theory then?"

"We are looking for a man with a very large, very well-trained dog," she hypothesized.

He uncle smiled proudly. "Please, go on."

"This man hunts these women," she explained. "He watches them, tracks them, and then when he is ready to kill, he sends his dog to take them down. That is why there are no screams. Then, once the dog has them by the throat, the man comes in and slashes them to pieces."

"And why do you believe the man is the one doing the slashing?"

"The wounds themselves," she explained. "The doctor noted how clean they were. No dirt, or debris. Just clean gashes. If it were an animal making those deep cuts, they would not have left the wound without dirt. Especially if that animal were a wolf or of canine descent as their claws never retract and, therefore, have all manner of dirt and filth under them. None of this was more evident than in poor Missy Hodgkin as she was found sooner than any of the other victims."

Her uncle clapped. "Bravo, my dear!" he exulted. "The only question now is 'whom' that animalistic man might be."

She frowned, thinking.

"Mr. Mackland has very large dogs, does he not?" her uncle asked slowly. "And it was rather convenient that this should have happened while you were out meeting with him."

Agrippina did not reply for several seconds. "I thought you did not like Mr. Mackland for these murders?"

He nodded. "True, but I do not believe in coincidences. Maybe one, or even two, but the amount we have come across is staggering."

She nodded. "I do not know. There is something off about it," she replied softly. "I am still missing something, uncle." She huffed in frustration.

"You seemed convinced enough yesterday, and you obviously still felt so this morning with wanting to leave his house in such a hurry."

"Yes, but it is almost too convenient," she explained. "I am teetering on the fence. One thought brings me closer to thinking it is him and the other makes me think it is not."

Dr. Greystone held his hand out, gesturing for her to continue.

"For one, he saved me. Why should he save me if I am the one that is trying to prove that he is guilty? The other side to that is, he faked the whole thing in order to save me so I would not suspect him anymore." She gently held her forearm against her as it began to throb again.

Dr. Greystone nodded slowly. "I see the conundrum you are in."

She shook her head. "But who else could have put something in my drink?" she asked. "The barmaid, I suppose had access, but to what purpose? What good would that have done her?" She thought back to the pub and the other people there. Out of the twenty or so patrons, she only knew three.

She sighed trying to think, but her head began to hurt again and she closed her eyes.

"I think a nice cup of tea and some rest would set you up right," her uncle told her.

She nodded. "I can hardly think without my head pounding."

He reached across and placed his hand gently on her knee. "You gave me quite a scare," he told her with feeling. "When I received Mr. Mackland's letter, I was sure you had been killed." He shook his head. "I do not know how I could have borne it if you were."

Agrippina put her hand on top of her uncle's. "Uncle, I—"

"I think we should return to Cambridge."

"What?" She frowned and shook her head. "How can you say that? We are so close to figuring this out. How could you just quit like that?"

"I almost lost you!" he shouted back. "Do you not understand that you are my only will to live?"

She started and blushed, her heart dropping at the pain in his voice.

"I know how dramatic that might seem, but you are my child. Niece by blood, but my child in every other respect." His voice shook with emotion. "If I lost you—" He stopped, unable to finish the thought.

"Uncle," she said softly after a brief silence, "I understand your feeling, but I am too stubborn to stop now. You said so yourself that I am practically unbearable when I cannot figure something out! How would you bear the two-week journey back to Cambridge if I have yet to solve these murders?"

He shook his head. "I cannot allow it," he whispered.

Agrippina huffed. "No, you cannot stop me."

He looked at her in surprise.

"I love you, uncle, and I respect you more than anyone I know or will ever meet, but I cannot run away from this. It is more important than me."

Her uncle looked too angry to reply.

"When did you or my father ever step away from a case?" she asked. "When was there a time you gave up because the stakes were too high?" She did not wait for him to answer. "Never! Is that not right? You and my father were determined and stubborn and sure of yourselves and your abilities. Well, so am I!" She nodded in her conviction. "And I have a right to finish what I have started. I have a right to see this through."

Her uncle laid back in his seat and looked at her, seeing the determination in her looks. "I am too weak to be of use," he told her. "What if you are attacked again?"

She thought for a moment. "I will employ Mr. Hodgkin to come with me. He knows almost everyone and he obviously knows his way around town. I am sure he would not say no to the money."

He nodded. "Why could you not bring Lord Beresford?"

She blinked at her uncle.

"He is an educated man; he could help you."

The carriage jolted, coming to an abrupt stop, causing them both to shift in their seats.

Agrippina opened the window and stuck her head out to see what was the matter. "Maybe we should discuss this later," she said opening the door and stepping out.

"Where are you going?" her uncle asked after her.

But Agrippina did not reply as she quickly walked up to the gathered crowd blocking the road. They seemed agitated as they whispered amongst themselves. She pushed her way through the outer circle until she was met with the grim face of the vicar.

"What is going on?" she asked seeing a cart carrying a body covered by a sheet. She frowned. "What has happened?"

"See for yourself, my lady, if you dare," Vicar Harmon replied, not holding back his bitterness.

Agrippina could feel herself tremble at his words, but she put on a brave face as she approached the cart. She slowly reached out and took the bloody sheet in her hand, taking a deep breath as she pulled it down. She gasped as she looked into the dead eyes of the barmaid from the Rose Bud, the barmaid that served her and Mr. Mackland their drinks.

She dropped the sheet, taking a step back. For a moment, she couldn't take her eyes off the poor young woman, but when she did, they were met with those of Robert Carne, and he appeared to be scowling at her.

18

HARRIET CARNE WAS A YOUNG WOMAN OF TWENTY WHO CAME to a tragic fate. Her body was not completely different from those of the other girls save for the bite mark. Agrippina noticed it right away that the only injuries appeared to be the slash marks. Though they had not been directed at her face as the other victims' wounds had been.

According to witnesses, Miss Carne left the Rose Bud not long after Mr. Mackland came back to look for Agrippina. She spoke with him briefly, stating that Agrippina had left. Witnesses did not recall seeing her after that. Some of the witnesses even claimed to have seen her leave after Mr. Mackland; others hadn't been so sure when she left.

"She was obviously attacked after me," Agrippina surmised as they finally made the last leg of the journey back to the inn. "That would account for the lack of bite mark."

"Do you think you killed the beast when you stabbed it?" her uncle asked.

She nodded after thinking for a moment. "I do. I know I landed the blade in a soft area. I could feel it." Her stomach churned as she remembered. "It was a sickening feeling."

They both sat in thoughtful silence until the carriage came to a safe stop in front of their inn. Lord Beresford, waiting by a window, rushed out to greet them.

"Miss Greystone!" he exclaimed. "You had me worried sick! When I saw your uncle's note this morning, I am sure I did not know what to do with myself. Luckily, he had another letter sent updating me on your recovery or I do not know what I would have done!"

She nodded. "Thank you, Thomas, for your concern," she replied with a small smile.

"Were you truly attacked?" he asked. "If that is the case, Dr. Greystone, could you not convince her to give this whole thing up and return back to Cambridge?"

"Ah, Lord Beresford, that is easier said than done I am afraid. My niece is not to be convinced. She will not hear of returning and is quite determined to see this thing through." He looked at his niece and smiled softly. "And, I daresay she will be most intolerable if she does not, stubborn thing that she is."

Lord Beresford looked bewildered but said no more.

"My uncle is right," Agrippina stepped in. "I especially cannot leave when there has been another murder."

Lord Beresford's eyes bulged. "Another murder?"

She nodded. "Yes, a barmaid. I saw her last night. She had been the one who served me my drink." Agrippina furrowed her brow pensively, thinking back to the Rose Bud and everyone who had been there the night before.

"Does that not unsettle you?" Lords Beresford looked at her, astonished.

"Yes, it was rather surprising considering I saw her alive last night and then saw her deceased body not fifteen minutes ago."

"You saw her?"

"Uncle, we should prepare ourselves for the vicar. We both know he is coming."

Dr. Greystone nodded. "Yes, I am sure he is. I will ask Mrs. Bragg for some tea." He nodded to Lord Beresford and left the room.

Agrippina, a little fatigued, walked to a sofa and sat down.

"That woman," Lord Beresford said, his voice heightened.

"I beg your pardon?"

"The old woman from yesterday who passed out right here." He pointed to the spot in question.

"Bertie?" Agrippina shook her head slightly. "What about her?"

"What about her?" he repeated in agitation. "She said before you left that you would meet with the devil! She warned you to be careful and then you were attacked!" He held his arms out in front of him as if telling her to look.

Agrippina felt a chill ripple through her, but she shook her head, downplaying the point he was trying to make. "You are trying to say there is a correlation between her warning and what happened to me?"

"Yes!"

"I cannot pretend to be that ridiculous, Thomas!" she exclaimed, faking a small laugh. "Bertie has said things similar to that effect since my uncle and I have arrived and I am sure she has made such gesticulations before and will make them after we leave."

"Gesticulations!" Lord Beresford pressed a hand to his forehead. "Good God, woman!" he sighed. "Our years apart have blinded me, made me forget how frustrating you are."

Agrippina frowned. "That is a little uncalled for."

"No, it is exactly what you need to hear, Aggy." He stood tall and took a deep breath, letting it out slowly. "Your uncle has allowed you to think and do as you please without correction."

She blanched at his mode of speech. "How dare you!"

"I am not done," he told her. "It is true, you are one of the most brilliant minds I have ever met, certainly the smartest woman I shall ever meet, but you fail to see past anything you deem illogical." He threw his hands in the air. "Ah, if it cannot be read in a book, or proven in a lab, or seen with your eyes, it is not real! It does not exist! It does not happen!" He shook his head. "Take off the blinders of academia, Aggy, and look!"

She blinked, half angry, half embarrassed. She clenched and unclenched her hands in agitation, trying to release the tension she felt building, but she did not reply—could not reply.

He took a deep breath and let it out slowly, running his fingers through his hair. "Forgive me," he said in a softer tone. "I do not wish to demean you the way I have seen other men do. Disregarding you as just a woman." He approached her, kneeling in front of her, and took her hand in his.

Agrippina uttered a small gasp in surprise.

"Miss Greystone, my dear Aggy," Lord Beresford began in a whisper, "you cannot begin to understand my feelings for you. The feelings I have always had. For a long time, you have been the woman whom has had all of my affections and admiration."

Agrippina felt herself blush, the deep burn of embarrassment reddening her cheeks. "Thomas," she breathed, "this is not the time for such declarations."

He nodded, unable to meet her eye. "I know and I did not plan for it to go this way, but I must tell you—I have been dying to tell you—how you have affected me, molded me. Everything I do, I do with you in mind somehow or another. And, I know we have not seen each other for the past five or six years, but, regardless, I found you as the model to which I compare every woman I meet." Finally, he looked up at her, his eyes shimmering with feeling.

Agrippina shook from agitation, terrified that someone would walk in at any moment and see them.

"Is there no hope?" he asked, almost desperately.

"No hope?"

"For us?"

Agrippina stared at Lord Beresford, unable to speak when the sound of the parlor door opening stirred her and she quickly stood from the couch to move to the other side of the room. Lord Beresford stood as well, turning to face the door.

It was not the vicar as Agrippina had thought it would be, but Mr. Mackland. She felt herself blush deeper as the two men regarded one another.

"Mr. Mackland, what are you doing here?" she asked, her confusion apparent.

"I came to see how you were doing," he replied. "You left so suddenly this morning, I wanted to make sure you did not have a relapse."

She looked away a moment. "I am fine, thank you."

Lord Beresford cleared his throat.

"Forgive me," she said motioning to him. "Mr. Mackland, this is Lord Beresford. He is the one who thought of my uncle when you sent Lord Helston that letter."

The men bowed at one another.

"I am indebted to you then," Mr. Mackland told Lord Beresford. "I have full confidence in Dr. Greystone and Miss Greystone."

Lord Beresford gave a single nod. "We are old friends. Naturally, I could think of no one else more capable."

There was a pregnant pause as the men turned their

gazes on her. She fidgeted, wishing her uncle would hurry back.

"I have heard there had been another death," Mr. Mackland said, breaking the silence. "Is it true?"

Agrippina nodded. "Yes. Harriet Carne."

He frowned. "A relation to Robert and Rebecca?"

"Yes, Rebecca had told me that she was her cousin." She cleared her throat. "In short, Harriet Carne was the woman who served us our drinks last night at the Rose Bud."

Mr. Mackland blanched. "What? She was our barmaid?"

"She was found by the side of the road this morning," she continued. "She was in the same condition as the other women."

Mr. Mackland shook his head. "And you are sure it is the same woman?" he asked in a low voice.

"Yes, I saw her myself."

Lord Beresford looked from one to the other as they talked, regarding their behavior toward one another.

"There were several witnesses from last night that saw you return to the Rose Bud and talk to Miss Harriet," Agrippina told him.

He nodded. "Yes, I spoke to her. I asked her whether or not you had gone. She told me you had, so I thanked her and left. I would hardly call it a significant interaction."

"No, it is just strange because no one remembers seeing her after that."

Mr. Mackland shrugged subtly and shook his head. "I cannot tell you otherwise. My object was not her; it was finding you and apologizing, which I now realize I did not have the chance to do." He smiled weakly at her which Agrippina returned.

She looked over at Lord Beresford and saw how he was looking at her intently. She shifted uncomfortably

"I wonder if Robert and Rebecca know about their cousin yet."

Agrippina frowned. "Robert does," she replied. "I saw him there, in the crowd of people trying to see what was going on. By the look on his face, he knew."

Mr. Mackland nodded solemnly. "There has been too much unnecessary death recently. I do not know how our little town will recover."

"I am sure they will find a way," Lord Beresford said, cutting in. "People are more resilient than you give them credit for."

Just then, Dr. Greystone came into the room, looking rather worried.

"What is it, Uncle?" Agrippina asked. "What is the matter?"

He cleared his throat and forced a small smile. "There appears to be a mob coming this way," he told them.

"What?" the other three in the room said in almost perfect unison.

Dr. Greystone nodded. "You were not wrong about the vicar coming," he said to his niece. "You just did not account for the number of guests he would be bringing with him."

"A mob? Are you sure?" Mr. Mackland asked.

"What could they want?" Lord Beresford added.

"Where is Bertie?" Agrippina cried.

"She is safe," Dr. Greystone replied calmly. "I have hidden her."

"Oh, oh, Dr. Greystone, sir!" wailed Mrs. Bragg as she came into the room. "They're practically at the door! What're we to do! I swear I've ne'er been so scared in all me life!"

"Calm yourself, woman," Dr. Greystone replied sternly. "There is no time for hysterics. Now, you and my niece will stay in here while the three of us go and see what the matter is."

"Uncle, no!" Agrippina exclaimed. "I should be out there as well. I am no good to anyone in here."

He uncle gave her a stern look. "I am not asking you, Agrippina. You will stay in here with Mrs. Bragg and you will make sure Bertie does not come out. That is what I need you for."

Agrippina held in a huff as she looked away but nodded.

"I made tea, miss," Mrs. Bragg informed her as if that would make her feel better. "I shall get it directly." She scampered off before anyone could say otherwise.

Lord Beresford cleared his throat. "I, uh, I think we should get out there," he said from the window. "They look rather unsettled. If we keep them waiting too long, they might start throwing things through the windows."

"Come then," Mr. Mackland replied, giving one last glance at Agrippina. "I would hate for them to damage anything of Mrs. Bragg's."

A strange sense of fear gripped at Agrippina's stomach as she watched the three of them go. She rushed to the window and pulled the sheer back slightly so she could see. Vicar Harmon, of course, was in the front of the mob which might have consisted of fifteen people. It was a sad mob to be sure, but Agrippina could see several muskets among its participants.

A small mob or not, they came armed, and they meant business.

She scanned the faces, seeing Mr. Marks and Harold Mellows among those in the crowd.

"Vicar Harmon!" Mr. Mackland bellowed from the stoop. "What brings you and these fine people of Blindburn to Mrs. Bragg's inn?"

"Here you go, miss," Mrs. Bragg whispered handing her a cup of tea.

Agrippina jumped, not having heard her slip back into the room. She did not feel as if it were the occasion for tea, but she smiled and thanked her, taking her cup.

"We came for the woman!" Vicar Harmon shouted.

Agrippina paled.

"What woman?" Mr. Mackland retorted.

"Lady Greystone!"

Agrippina could just see her uncle, Lord Beresford, and Mr. Mackland start from where they stood in front of the door.

"Why should you come for her?" Dr. Greystone spoke this time. "We did not come until after the murders. My niece has nothing to do with this."

"We have heard she was bitten by the beast!" shouted someone in the crowd.

"She has been cursed!" cried another.

"She will turn at the next full moon!" came a third.

The vicar silenced them and turned back to the house. "She bears the mark of the beast now and will be controlled by it. We must take her into custody as no one is safe while she is free."

"That is absurd!" Lord Beresford yelled.

"My niece was bitten by nothing more than a dog!" Dr. Greystone shouted calmly. "There is no need for any of this!

Vicar Harmon turned his unbelieving eyes on him. "She will not be harmed! I give you my word. And once the true monster behind all of this is put to death, she will be free from his power and released."

"Vicar," Mr. Mackland began, "as much as I respect your opinion on all things ecclesiastical, I do not—I cannot— approve your reasoning for this."

The vicar gave a smug smirk. "Well, then I doubt you will approve what we are about to do next." He raised a hand

and those in the crowd with guns raised them.

Agrippina gasped, dropping her tea and running to the front door. She flew open the door and pushed her way through the three men standing there with their hands raised.

The three of them shouted simultaneously when they saw her. Lord Beresford reached for her, but she stepped forward too far.

"Stop! Please!" she shouted. "Put down your weapons! There is no need for violence!"

"Move out of the way," Vicar Harmon ordered, coldly.

"I will go willingly! Just, please, put down your weapons!"

"Agrippina!" her uncle shouted behind her. "No!"

"The guns are not for you," the vicar told her. "They are for him." He pointed behind her and she turned, seeing a set scowl on Mr. Mackland's face. "We are here to arrest him for the crime of lycanthropy and the murder of those women."

She shook her head, knowing, feeling, at that moment that he was innocent. She could not explain why she felt that way; every woman murdered had some connection with him either by first degree of separation, or by two. Regardless, she knew it was not him and whatever she was missing would prove that.

"No!" she vociferated, running back to Mr. Mackland and standing in front of him. "You are wrong!" She shook her head. "It is not Mr. Mackland."

Vicar Harmon narrowed his eyes at her. "We heard it on good authority that you thought it was him yourself."

Agrippina was confused; the only person she had spoken to about her suspicions, other than outwardly accusing Mr. Mackland herself, was her uncle, and she knew he had not told anyone."

"I was wrong!" she admitted. "He is not guilty."

"Then who is?" angrily shouted a few men from the crowd.

"How very convenient of you to change your mind after you have been bitten," the vicar pointed out.

She frowned. "That has nothing to do with it! I know it is not him!" She turned slightly so she could look at him. "I believe it is someone else. I just have not figured out who, yet."

"Mr. Mackland, you can either come with us civilly, or you can provoke us to arrest you uncivilly," the vicar said, the guns still raised, the sound of the men pulling the hammers back to full cocked positions rippling fear through Agrippina.

"No!" she yelled again.

Mr. Mackland wrapped his arms around her waist and spun them both a hundred and eighty degrees so that she was no longer standing between him and the muskets. He held her tight for a moment as she squirmed.

"What are you doing? They will kill you!" she told him.

"And your standing in front of me will not prevent them from trying," he whispered into her ear. "Desperate men do desperate things, Miss Greystone."

She stopped struggling as he slowly let go and turned back to face the mob. She stood, facing away, her body frozen until her uncle pulled her close to him.

"I am not the man you want," he began, "but I will not incite violence to disprove what you so heartily believe."

"Do it, vicar!" someone shouted. "Reveal the fur beneath his skin!"

"Do it!" shouted the other men.

Mr. Mackland frowned. "Is that why you have come?" he shouted above the cries for justice. "Do you wish to cut me? To see if I should bleed like an ordinary man?" He rolled up his sleeves and pulled a small knife from his boot. "Do you wish to cut me open in the hopes of seeing the fur beneath it revealed?" He pressed the knife to his wrist and raked it across, allowing a river of blood to flow from it.

Agrippina gasped, not at the sight of blood, but at seeing Mr. Mackland willingly cut himself in demonstration.

"Come! Look!" he demanded. "Come and see that I am clean!" He took a few steps forward. "Look! Does this not prove my innocence?"

"'Tis a trick!" Harold Mellows cried. "He wishes to fool us!"

Vicar Harmon snarled. "Calm yourselves!" He took a step closer and took Mr. Mackland by the wrist examining the cut. "It is a clean wound," he surmised, dropping his arm. "But that doesn't mean anything. There are more tests you have to pass before we believe you."

"No, they mean to torture him, uncle!" Agrippina cried, pleadingly. "We cannot let them take him."

Lord Beresford looked over at her, seeing the desperation in her eyes and frowned.

"What 'bout the woman?" Mr. Marks asked. "We can' leave 'er to transform and take over for 'im."

"No!" Mr. Mackland bellowed. "I will go willingly, but only if you do not take Miss Greystone. The next full moon is not for another month. There can be no harm leaving her be until then. Do whatever you wish to me, but leave her out of it."

"Shackle him!" Vicar Harmon ordered.

"No!" Lord Beresford said, stepping forward. "There will be none of that." He reached into his jacket pocket and pulled out a rolled-up piece of paper. "This notice gives me the authority from King George himself in this investigation. No interrogations of this man will be conducted without me being present. If I hear that he has been harmed in any way, I will personally have you escorted to the Tower of London."

There was an uncomfortable whisper that made its way through the mob, all of their determined faces looking less confident.

"With all due respect, sir," Vicar Harmon replied, narrowing his eyes, "I have been told this lie before."

Lord Beresford narrowed his eyes in return. "Does this seal look like a lie to you?" He held the paper out for the vicar to see who blanched upon seeing it. "This man is a gentleman, and he shall be treated with the respect due his rank."

Vicar Harmon huffed. "Forgive me, sir, but we lack a cell with a canopy bed."

"Then he shall be put on house arrest."

"That is absurd!"

Lord Beresford held up his hand, stopping him from talking anymore. "I shall personally oversee his incarceration along with some of your most trusted men."

The vicar turned and looked at the men behind him. "Mr. Marks and Harold Mellows then," he replied. "They shall assist you with the prisoner."

The two men stepped forward with sneers on their faces as they each took Mr. Mackland by an arm.

"I'll gladly do so," Mr. Marks said, glaring into the defiant face of Mr. Mackland.

"You all will now disperse," Lord Beresford commanded. "There is no need for violence. Mr. Mackland will be brought to justice, but under the civilized law of our country."

The men lingered for a few more moments until the vicar waved them away, leaving satisfied but somewhat suspicious of the one giving orders.

"I will hold you responsible from here on out, sir," Vicar

Harmon told him shooting a glare at Agrippina and pointing at her. "For that woman as well."

Lord Beresford caught the vicar by the wrist. "You forget yourself, sir," he growled.

The vicar swallowed hard.

"Return to your flock, vicar." Lord Beresford dropped his wrist and walked away meeting the eyes of Agrippina whose cheeks were wet with tears.

She thanked him graciously, but it was a bitter feeling to him. He merely nodded and ushered his new ward to his carriage. Agrippina stepped away from her uncle and stared on as the men drove away, Mr. Mackland just visible through the window of the carriage.

19

AGRIPPINA PACED HER ROOM, AGITATED AND FLUSTERED BY the morning's events. Every few minutes she would sigh and shake her head as she came up again and again with nothing. What was she missing? How did the vicar know she had suspected Mr. Mackland? How did they know she had been bitten?

She tucked a loose piece of hair behind her ear and made her way back to the window to look out at nothing. She then moved to the desk and rustled through her notes, skimming through a page here or there before moving away again.

Her heart fluttered nervously as she thought about the gravity of Mr. Mackland's situation and a flush spread over her cheeks. She pressed a hand to her face and shook her head once again.

Mr. Mackland was innocent. She realized that, but what had made her think so?

Her forearm throbbed and she looked down at it, gently wrapping her hand around the wound. After a moment, she looked back up, realizing what had made her release Mr. Mackland in her mind. His dogs. Hubert and Angeline. They were both fine that morning when she saw them. They were both alive. No bandages or wounds.

She looked through her notes to the day she first met Mr. Mackland, nibbling her lip as she read until she found what she was looking for.

Admits to the inability to control his dogs. Says his game-keeper trains dogs for hunting.

She looked up again, her heart pounding.

Robert Carne.

It made sense. The first victim was the woman who rejected him. He killed her out of revenge and the others, the others were to cover his tracks or out of jealously. They were a reminder of the woman who took back her promise to marry him. The other women personalized his rejection all over again.

Her notes fell from her hands, scattering to the floor as she turned and ran from her room. She threw open the door and all but stumbled over Bertie who was just about to knock.

Agrippina exclaimed in surprise as she traversed to miss the old woman.

"Forgive me, miss," Bertie apologized. "I'd not mean to scare ye."

"It is all right, Bertie," Agrippina told her, pressing her hand to her pounding heart. "What is wrong?"

"I come to check on ye," she said reaching out to take Agrippina's arm. She frowned when she saw the bandages. "A poor mess they made of ye arm."

Agrippina regarded the old woman as she examined her arm. "Bertie," she began slowly and quietly, "those other times when you warned me about the devil, do you know who it was you were warning me against?"

Bertie looked up from Agrippina's wrist. "The devil is the

devil, miss," she told her matter-of-factly.

"But those times you warned me."

"'e uses others to do 'is work. The devil be lazy."

"Do you know who?" Agrippina pressed. "Do you know who he uses?"

"'e uses us all. Some more than others, mind ye."

"And Robert Carne? Is that someone he uses more than others?"

"Carne?" Bertie repeated in almost a gravelly whisper as her eyes began a distant stare.

Agrippina gave a small gasp as she watched the old woman's eyes darken.

"Carne!" she said again, her now dark eyes wide. "Carne, I know ye well. I know thee blackness of thine soul, the brokenness of thine 'eart. 'Tis Carne who made thee pact with thee devil."

"Thank you, Bertie," Agrippina said, taking the old woman by the arm as her trance ended.

The woman gave a weak smile. "So nice o' ye, miss," she replied, allowing her to guide her to a seat.

Agrippina kissed Bertie's hand. "Rest. Regain your strength." She then knocked on her uncle's door, whose muffled coughs could just be heard through the thick wood. After a moment she opened the door on her own to see her uncle on the floor, leaning against a chair.

She ran to him, helping him back up.

"What a sad state you find me in," he said, a somber smile on his face. He wiped the blood from his lips as she sat him in the chair he had been leaning on.

"Oh, uncle," she sighed.

He waved a hand. "Do not begin with your lamentations," he warned her. "I want nothing of them." He relaxed more into the chair. "This morning was more excitement than I needed, I suppose."

"Let me call for Dr. Johns," she begged. "He could at least give you something to help alleviate your coughing."

He shook his head. "All I need is some tea and honey. Have Mrs. Bragg bring some to me, but first, tell me why you came in here all excited?"

"Uncle, you were in no condition to tell how I was feeling when I entered."

He gave a weak chuckle. "It was in the way you knocked," he told her. "You figured something out."

She smiled, a little embarrassed at how well he knew her. "Yes," she replied quietly.

"Well, what are you waiting for? Tell me, my dear, tell me!"

Agrippina nodded and relayed to her uncle her new theory. "Only a well-trained dog could attack on command and Mr. Mackland himself admitted how horrible he is with commanding his dogs. But his gamekeeper, Mr. Carne, trains his dogs for hunting."

Her uncle looked intrigued. "Why would he attack the sheep?"

She thought for a moment. "We had let Bertie go," she explained. "She was his scapegoat, his way out. He had to make it appear as if, by her being free, she was able to kill again. And, he must have heard me accuse Mr. Mackland and then spread it around town!"

She paced the room, taking quick breaths as her excitement grew.

"What are you thinking, Agrippina?" her uncle asked her, knowing what was coming.

"I have to go," she replied, stopping. "I have to get Robert Carne."

Her uncle struggled up from the chair. "You will do no such thing on your own!" he ordered. "You nearly died last night."

She nodded. "I know, but if I do not do something, Mr. Mackland could die."

"You will alert the proper authorities! At least bring someone with you!"

She hesitated but nodded. "The only person I trust is Lord Beresford. I will ride to Mr. Mackland's and retrieve him before I go and find Carne."

He eyed her skeptically.

"Oh, uncle, honestly!" she yelled. She rushed over to him and kissed his forehead. "I will not go alone I promise, but I must hurry!"

He nodded. "Retrieve my bag." He pointed to the item in question.

She quickly gathered it and handed it to him.

He opened the bag and rummaged around in a side pocket until he pulled a pistol out.

Agrippina looked down at it wide eyed. "You have a gun, uncle?"

He handed it to her which she took tentatively. "I had been correct in giving you a knife. It, without a doubt, saved your life. You lost your knife, and are once again in need of a weapon. Use it wisely."

She nodded.

He sighed. "Be careful, my dear."

She stared down at the gun in her hand for a moment before tucking it into her garter. "I will." And, with one last look at her uncle, she left.

20

Agrippina jumped off the horse in front of Mackland Manor and knocked on the door. Her anxiety and anticipation were rising with every passing second. Finally, after what seemed like forever, the door was opened by Rebecca who seemed a little more disheveled than usual.

"Oh, miss," she said with her awkward curtsey. "I'm real glad yer 'ere. I'm so confused, ye can' imagine. These strange men be holdin' Mr. Mackland as if he be a prisoner, like a common crim'nal!"

Agrippina nodded. "Yes, I know, Rebecca," she replied, a little impatiently. "I am here to talk to one of those men. Lord Beresford. Would you tell him I am here to speak to him please?"

"Aye, miss, right away!"

"And I am very sorry to hear about your cousin," Agripinna told her in a softer tone.

Rebecca's eyes took on a somber light and her lips twitched into a sad smile. "Mighty kind of ye, miss, to say so. She were always kind to me." She turned to leave.

"Oh, Rebecca, is your brother on the grounds?"

Rebecca blinked at her a moment before shaking her head. "No, miss, I belie'e 'e didn' come in today."

"Thank you, Rebecca."

Rebecca hobbled off to retrieve Lord Beresford and Agrippina took notice of the several tears in her dress that seemed new. She forgot about them, however, when Lord Beresford met her in the foyer.

"Miss Greystone," he said as he rushed down the stairs. "What on earth are you doing here?"

"I believe I have figured out who the real murderer is," she whispered. "And, you are the only person I trust to come with me to make the arrest."

"Should you not have asked the local magistrate to go with you?" he asked.

Agrippina was taken aback by his response. "Did you not hear me?" she retorted. "I said you are the only one I trust."

"Which is why I am here looking after Mr. Mackland," he replied a little bitterly.

She frowned. "I apologize for the inconvenience, but your gallantry was purely voluntary. Now, if you do not come with me to arrest the man whom I think is actually responsible for these heinous crimes, then I shall go alone." She lifted up her skirts and pulled the gun from her garter startling Lord Beresford. "It has been a few years since we shot bottles off the fences on your father's estate, but I am sure it is very much the same."

"Uh—uh—" He cleared his throat. "Miss Greystone, if I recall, you were not the best shot."

She shrugged. "Yes, but I plan to be closer to this target."

He huffed. "I will go, but only if you give *me* the gun."

She lifted a brow at him but complied. "Deal." She handed the gun over willingly. "Hurry up then." She turned sharply and led him out the door.

"Miss Greystone!" he called after her. "Are you first going to tell me where it is we are going?"

She pointed to a little house not two hundred yards away. "Now, we better hurry." She got back on her horse leaving room for Lord Beresford to climb on as well.

He blushed as he climbed on behind her, the smell of her hair filling his nostrils as he took the reins and drove them forward.

THE SMALL HOUSE WAS QUAINTLY LOCATED ON A SMALL knoll facing the valley to the front and the River Coquet just visible from the back. Lord Beresford got off the horse, holding a hand out for Agrippina. She took it absent-mindedly as she slid down and walked toward the front of the house.

"Will you wait?" Lord Beresford whispered harshly, coming up behind her.

She ignored him as she knocked on the door.

They stood, waiting in anticipation, but no one answered. She knocked again, but there was still no answer.

Growing impatient, Agrippina opened the door and stepped in, the light from the late afternoon sun barely letting in enough light to see. She took a few steps, squinting in the darkness.

"Mr. Carne?" Agrippina called out, a little unsure. "Mr. Carne, are you here?"

"Do you smell that?" Lord Beresford said beside her, gun at his side. "Smells rather metallic."

She sniffed tentatively and nodded. "Yes." She walked over to the window and threw open the shabby curtains, letting in more light.

"Good God!" Lord Beresford exclaimed.

Agrippina whipped around and started, seeing a slumped body in the corner of the room sitting in a pool of blood. She rushed over to it, her skin prickling with fear.

"Miss Greystone!" Lord Beresford exclaimed, trying to stop her from getting any closer, but it was no use.

Agrippina knelt by the body and realized what she already knew. It was Robert Carne. She fell back on her haunches and let out a small sob as she saw the unmistakable slash mark across his chest, his droplets of blood splattered all around him.

"No! No! It cannot be him!" She shook her head. "This does not make any sense."

Lord Beresford placed a hand on her shoulder and squeezed it reassuringly before kneeling beside her.

"How could this have happened?" She buried her face in her hands with a groan and shook her head again.

"He does not appear to have been dead long." Lord Beresford nudged Robert Carne with his boot. "This blood has barely dried."

"No, you are right, I saw him this morning."

"Hm." Lord Beresford walked off, observing the small room.

"I do not understand" she whispered to herself. "I missed something. I must have missed something. I was so sure it was him, but—"

"Miss Greystone," Lord Beresford said softly.

She looked up and saw Lord Beresford standing in front of the back window. She got up from the floor and hurried over to him. Outside, a few yards from the house, was the outstretched body of a dog, a stain matting its wiry grey fur.

Agrippina rushed out the back door to the dog and stopped when she was a few feet away. There, on the ground, next to the dog's body, was the knife her uncle had given her. The knife she used to stab the dog when it attacked her.

"I was partially correct," she whispered, hearing Lord Beresford coming up beside her. "Robert Carne's dog was used in the attacks. But it is obvious he was not involved beyond that." She shook her head. "He might not have even known someone was using his dog."

"Who else could have?"

Agrippina frowned letting out a sigh. "I do not know. There is his sister, but she does not have the strength capable of performing these murders. She can barely walk; she takes pain relievers and sleeping aids to—" She stopped, scanning her thoughts.

"What are you thinking?"

She shook her head. "It cannot be." She went back into the house, Lord Beresford right behind her. She burst back inside and searched what little belongings they had. She rummaged through the rooms, opening boxes, looking under their beds, and in drawers to wardrobes.

"What are you looking for?" Lord Beresford asked her.

"The murder weapon," she replied with a sigh as she came up with nothing. "Or something." She gave a huff when she had yet to yield anything.

Lord Beresford stepped into the small room and shook his head. "It would be easier to find if I knew what you were looking for."

She scanned the room with her eyes for the hundredth time. "Something that emulates claws or something."

He walked toward the bed and lifted the thin mattress and found a small brown bottle. "What is this?" He held it up, examining it for a moment before opening it and sniffing it tentatively. He coughed and scrunched his face up unpleasantly.

She walked over to him and took the bottle smelling it as

well. She resisted the urge to gag, but the smell immediately brought the whiskey from last night to mind. This bottle, however, was still full.

"What is this on the ground?" Lord Beresford asked, pointing to a worn-out area in the wooden floor.

Agrippina turned her attention to it and frowned. She moved about the house, studying the floors, seeing similar marks throughout. "They seem to be drag marks."

She stood still, visions of the case flashing through her mind. The image of the single bite mark, clean wounds, a drag trail by the sheep's bodies, the dog she caught a glimpse of at the Rose Bud.

"We need to get back to Mackland Manor," she said.

"But we have not found the murder weapon yet."

"We are not supposed to."

He frowned. "I do not understand."

"You will soon enough."

21

LORD BERESFORD, AT HIS INSISTENCE, OPENED THE DOOR TO Mackland Manor, gun out. He poked his head in to make sure the coast was clear before waving Agrippina in. They walked into the foyer cautiously looking around when they noticed the partially opened door to the parlor, the sounds of a crackling fire drifting from it. Lord Beresford motioned for Agrippina to stay behind him as they slowly moved toward it.

Lord Beresford pushed open the door the rest of the way with his foot and peered in. He had not taken two steps in, however, when a shadow moved to his right. He tried to avoid the attack, but was not fast enough, and the sound of something hard cracking into his skull reverberated through Agrippina's ears. She froze.

Agrippina took a few steps away from the door. "Rebecca?" she called out, trying to keep her voice from shaking. "Is that you?"

There wasn't an immediate response, but after a moment or two, Rebecca stepped into the doorway and smiled.

"Ah, miss, 'tis you!" she exclaimed. "I thought it be

someone come to murder me. You ne'er know these days."

Agrippina looked behind Rebecca at the motionless body of Lord Beresford on the floor. She wasn't sure if he was dead or unconscious from where she was standing, but she could not see him moving.

"Rebecca," Agrippina said slowly, "where are the other men?" She swallowed hard. "Are they upstairs?"

Rebecca's smile didn't leave her face, but only deepened. "Their bodies are," she replied nonchalantly.

Agrippina felt her stomach clench in fear and apprehension, tears welling in her eyes. "Are they all dead?"

"Not Mr. Mackland, no," she told her, sounding innocent. "'e's still in 'is study. Though 'e might be well asleep by now."

Agrippina felt a wave of relief wash over her. "What did you do to Mr. Marks and Mr. Mellows?"

Rebecca shrugged. "Why'd ya think I've done anythin'?"

"I saw your brother, Rebecca. I found him. Robert is dead, but you already knew that, did you not?"

The smile faded from her face. "I don' know what yer talkin' 'bout."

"You cannot play those innocent games with me!" Agrippina retorted. "You might have everyone else fooled, but not me. You might think you are safe behind your limp— behind your portrayed weakness. It is why you used your dog to help you. He chased down your victims, held them by the throat to give you time to catch up and kill them."

Rebecca stood taller, her smirk returning to her face. "Is that so?"

"Yes, your limp and weak demeanor are the perfect cover for who you really are. A monster."

Rebecca's expression remained unchanged.

"You were angry with Hannah Marks for breaking off the engagement with your brother. So angry that you decided to kill her. She was going to be your only victim, but you found out how much you love it. Killing. It was thrilling, made you feel powerful; made you feel better than them. All those women who used to feel sorry for you, look down on you. All of those pretty women who would do the one thing you never will, marry."

Rebecca was scowling at her, her eyes flashing red.

"You hated them," Agrippina continued, seeing how she was angering her. "You hated how pretty they were; resented them for it. So you wanted to take it away from them.

"'Poor Rebecca Carne,' they must have thought. Bringing you gifts of medicine, spreading their joy, bragging about the new lives they were about to start. You envied them; you wanted to be them. But you could not. Look at you! They were living angels and you are nothing more than a hairless dog that the men of this town have never looked twice at."

Rebecca let out a scream. "I deserve everythin' they 'ad! Hannah threw it away when she denied me brother. Broke 'is 'eart, but that was just the beginning. After 'er, I know what I needed to do. I needed to take out those women who took their good fortune fer granted!" She pulled from her dress pocket something that looked like wearable claws and slipped them onto her hand. "At first, I didn' intend to kill Hannah." She shook her head. "No, I only wanted to scare 'er. But the fury I ne'er known I 'ad took over me and I just couln' stop!" She held the claws up, the metal glistening in the sunlight shining through a window.

Rebecca laughed. "And it felt so good! Watching as her life slipped from 'er, 'er eyes startin' to haze over." .

"So, you used your brother's dog to hunt them down while you trailed behind them on your pony. Once he had them by the throat, unable to scream, you killed them."

She sneered. "I almost killed you last night too 'ad you not been knocked out. 'Tis a shame. Seein' the fear in thee eyes 'tis the best part. But I couldn' do that wi' you. That bump on yer 'ead saved yer life. That an' thee shouts o' Mr. Mackland."

Agrippina shuddered.

There was a groan behind them and Rebecca turned slightly to see what it was. Agrippina took this opportunity to tackle her, causing her to squeal, one of the clawed weapons flying from her hand and skidding across the marble floors. Agrippina grabbed a fistful of Rebecca's hair and slammed it against the floor just as her other hand tried slashing at her. Agrippina dodged the sharp blades, but just barely as it scratched at her arm and drew blood.

"Get off!" Rebecca yelled, throwing Agrippina from her with surprising strength.

Agrippina tumbled to the floor, quickly regaining herself as Rebecca lunged at her, slashing. Agrippina continued to evade her blows as Rebecca pushed her further away from the parlor door until her back was against a wall with nowhere else to go.

"I will cut your pretty face to pieces like I did to all thee others!" Rebecca cried as she raised her arm.

Before she could bring her arm down, however, a shot rang through the house. Confused, Rebecca stood there for a moment, motionless until she slowly turned her head to see a gaping wound in her shoulder. She let out a cry as she fell to the floor on her knees, pressing her hand to the wound to help staunch the flow of blood.

Agrippina looked up and saw Lord Beresford bracing himself on the doorframe, blood dripping down the side of his head, the pistol still raised. She rushed over to him.

"Thomas!" she exclaimed. "I thought you were dead!"

He smiled weakly as he slid down the doorframe and

plopped onto the floor. "My head might beg to differ," he groaned, finally dropping the gun and pressing a hand to his temple. "How bad is it?"

Agrippina gently tilted his head, causing him to wince. "It could be worse, but I would not be surprised if you felt the effects of this for a couple of weeks."

"Mmh."

"Stay here," she told him moving back to Rebecca, whose shoulder wound appeared worse at first than it actually was.

"They're gonna h-hang me f-fer this," she stuttered through the pain.

Agrippina nodded. "I would venture to say you deserve it."

Rebecca shook her head. "N-no, no! What I did w-was right. *They* deserved it. They was ungrateful for what they 'ad."

"And your cousin and brother? What did they do to deserve it?"

She sneered again.

"They both found out, did they not? Harriet after you laced my drink at the Rose Bud and Robert after he found his dog dead."

Rebecca did not reply; she merely narrowed her eyes at Agrippina.

"Whatever excuse you might have, Rebecca," Agrippina told her with indifference, "nothing could convince me that your actions have been justified."

Rebecca scowled. "My master would say otherwise," she growled.

Agrippina frowned and took a step back. "Mr. Mackland?"

Rebecca cackled. "Mr. Mackland is not my master."

A chill ran down Agrippina's spine.

"'e would've loved to add ye to our collection." She cackled again as she pulled down the neck of her dress to reveal the scar of what looked like a bite mark. "'e might not 'ave ye now, but 'e'll be seein' ye soon 'nough."

"The mark of the devil," Lord Beresford whispered from behind Agrippina, causing her to jump. "That is her master. He gave her the strength she needed."

Agrippina shook her head, but she was too confused and shocked to reply. A pact with the devil. How could that be possible?

Rebecca continued to laugh at her confusion, a sound that would ring through Agrippina's ears for years to come.

AFTER REBECCA HAD BEEN SECURED, AGRIPPINA WENT upstairs and found the bodies of Mr. Marks and Harold Mellows outside the door to Mr. Mackland's room, an over-turned drink—laced with whatever was slipped her the other day, no doubt—on the ground beside them. If it had not been for the gaping wounds in their necks, Agrippina would have thought they were just passed out.

Tentatively, and apprehensively, she opened the door to the room where Mr. Mackland had been bound and gagged. His head jerked up lazily when he saw her, blood beginning to dry to the side of his face.

She ran to him and took the gag off, examining his head wound.

"Rebecca!" he uttered breathlessly. "It is her!"

Agrippina nodded. "It is all right," she told him as she began to undo the ropes. "She is not going to hurt anyone ever again."

He collapsed to the floor as she released the final rope with a dull thud and a groan. She propped his head onto her lap and brushed his cheek.

"Mr. Mackland," she half cried.

"You saved me," he breathed, looking up at her, his eyes half glazed over, "again."

Agrippina's stomach knotted and her cheeks flushed as she looked down at him, his eyes fluttering heavily. She brushed back a lock of his hair that had fallen across his face as he fell asleep peacefully on her lap.

Lord Beresford watched them from the doorway with a heavy heart. He shot them one last glance before he turned around and left the image of what he would never have with Agrippina behind him.

22

Rebecca Carne screamed and yelled when they dragged her away, thrashing about like a wild animal. She confessed to it all without the threat of torture, laughing as she did so.

She reveled in the shock she was met with when she told and retold her tale, adding more horrific details as she went along. However she might have embellished the murders the more she retold them, there was one aspect that remained the same; how she came to be a mistress to the devil.

Her eyes glistened as she spun a tale that brings chills to every God-fearing Christian's heart. She told them how, after Hannah Marks had broken her engagement with her brother, she was walking in the woods with her dog, Linus. She had stumbled and fallen to the ground as her leg was weak.

She cursed the Lord for giving her such a feeble body. She crawled to her knees and prayed for strength, for some sort of redemption to fall upon her. That was when she heard a voice. It started as a growl, but soon enough, the words became more audible.

When she looked up, she saw the shadow of a man

approaching her. The figure was tall, though she could not see any facial features. The sight of him was terrifying and yet she felt no fear as he spoke to her.

He had offered her great things; he told her he could give her the proper use of her leg; he offered her strength and ability; he offered her power she could have never dreamed of.

And she took it.

She took it without even hearing what she had to deliver in return.

And it was right there, on the forest floor, where she sealed the deal, and gave her body and soul to that shadowy figure. It was then—in the heat of their forbidden passion—that he bit her, leaving the scar on the shoulder.

It was only afterwards did she know he required blood and sacrifice.

From then on, she met that shadowy figure in the woods to give herself to him over and over, giving him the blood he desired and he in turn made the pain in her leg subside. She belonged to him, and she did not regret it.

It was there that Georgina Wilkes found her on that fateful day. She had witnessed what Rebecca was doing. She had turned to run, but it was no use. That was why she had been attacked from behind, while the others merely walked into her trap willingly. Blind to the rage within her as she approached them, her dog Linus beside her.

She had enjoyed the killing, but she killed for the devil.

Agrippina listened to all of this with skepticism. This woman was not a witch, or mistress to the devil; she was insane. But that did not explain several unexplained issues she encountered while investigating.

No, it did not sit well with Agrippina to blame her murders on the will of some ethereal being, a monster, the devil.

She is the only one who should be blamed. Devil or not, she made the decision to do what she did. It was she who killed nine people, including her own cousin and brother. It was she who attacked her.

Regardless, Agrippina had to be satisfied. The case was over. The murderer had been caught and would soon be brought to justice and hung for her crimes. The devil could not save her from that.

When all was said and done, and the prisoner properly secured, it was time to leave. Agrippina sighed as she packed, feeling as if it had been a lifetime since she had seen her beloved Cambridge when there was a light rapping at her door.

She opened it and Lord Beresford bowed.

He cleared his throat. "I, uh, thought I should stay another day or two to make sure things are handled properly."

She nodded. "I am sure they will not appreciate it as much as it may be needed."

He gave a small laugh. "Also, I did not wish to make the ride back to Cambridge awkward."

Agrippina shifted her gaze to the floor. "I do not know why it should be, Thomas," she replied softly. "I will always think fondly of you."

"Ah, yes, but not in the way a man would wish a wife to think of him," he concluded without bitterness. He forced a smile. "I wish you well, Miss Greystone. Truly, I do. I wish you the world even if I am not the one to give it to you."

"We part as friends, then?"

He nodded. "We part as friends." He gave a deep bow. "Safe travels to you and your uncle. And, if you are ever in need of anything, please do not hesitate to ask. I am due the both of you more favors than I care to admit."

She thanked him and replied that she would think of him

first if she ever was in need.

He smiled, though somberly, and left.

Agrippina moved to the window as she heard a carriage pull up, and she frowned, worried that theirs came earlier than expected, but when she saw it was Mr. Mackland's her heart skipped a beat and a jolt of electricity coursed through her.

She stepped away from the window again lest he see her watching him and tried to resume what little packing she had left until there was another knock at her door. She smoothed out her dress and straightened her back before opening it. She was slightly disappointed, however, when she saw Mrs. Bragg on the other side.

"You've a visitor, miss. Mr. Mackland come to see you and yer uncle off."

Agrippina shot her a small smile. "Thank you. I will be down directly."

"D'ya need 'elp with packin'? I can finish it for ye."

She shook her head. "No, thank you. I only have a few things left and I am rather particular. It is best I finish on my own."

Mrs. Bragg looked disappointed not to be of help but smiled anyway. "All right then, miss. I shall tell Mr. Mackland you'll be down in a bit."

"Thank you, Mrs. Bragg."

Agrippina quickly gathered the rest of her things and dropped them in her remaining bag before she made her way downstairs where Bertie was serving tea in the parlor.

"Mrs. Bragg said she'll let me stay if I 'elp," she said proudly as she gently placed the tray on the table. "I tol' 'er, I be thee best 'elp she e'er 'ad!"

"I am glad to hear you will be well settled, Bertie," Dr. Greystone replied as he took the cup proffered to him. "I was thinking of offering you a place in our household as well."

"So nice ye are, sir," she told him with such feeling, "but this be me 'ome. 'Tis all I know." She gave a dip of her head and waddled past Agrippina, a grin on her face.

"Ah! There you are, Aggy my dear!" Dr. Greystone exclaimed as she entered the room. "Look who has come to see us away." He motioned with his hand to Mr. Mackland who stood from his chair to bow at her entrance.

She greeted him, though shyly at first. "How is your head?"

He subconsciously brought his hand to where Rebecca had hit him. "Much better, I thank you. Dr. Johns has given me a few remedies for the headaches. He says I might suffer a few over the next few weeks."

She nodded.

"I have been advised not to travel as well, but I could not leave without giving you both a proper goodbye." The statement was directed at Agrippina and her uncle, but his eyes never left hers while speaking.

"Well, we shall not tell Dr. Johns if you do not!" her uncle said, cutting in.

Mr. Mackland smiled and bowed slightly in his direction. "It is greatly appreciated if you do not. He can become rather cross when his directions are not followed to the letter."

"Ah, that goes with the profession, I am afraid. When I was a practicing doctor, before I returned to academia, I had my moments of crossness toward delinquent patients. I often grumbled about them."

Mr. Mackland laughed. "I cannot imagine you grumbling, sir."

"Careful, Mr. Mackland," Agrippina said in a light tone, "he will think you are giving him a compliment and then it will go to his head."

"My niece always knows when to ground me," he chuckled. "You know me too well, my dear."

Their carriage arrived just as they were finishing tea and their luggage was quickly packed. The men went outside to help direct the loading while Agrippina busied herself by taking in a few more moments in the parlor. It was a quaint little room, and she felt she would miss it with its peeling wallpaper, and gently stained rugs.

She was about to turn out of the room when Bertie walked in holding a bottle of what appeared to be wine.

"I made this for ye, miss," she said, extending her arm.

Agrippina gripped the bottle. "Is this wine, Bertie?" she asked, wondering where the old beggar woman would have gotten the money to buy wine.

She shook her head. "Nay, miss," she replied. "'Tis a witch bot'le."

Agrippina blinked at the gift. "Witch bottle?"

"To ward off evil spirits an' witches," Bertie explained.

Agrippina held it closer, trying to peer through the green glass at the contents. She could just make out the shadows of something floating around at the bottom. "What is in it?"

"'Tis uh mixture o' sorts." She nodded her head at the bottle. "But i' 'as some nails, some 'air I took from one o' yer brushes, a hint of wine, and me own urine."

Agrippina's eyes grew wide at the last ingredient.

"This will protect ye agains' witches. Keeps them away, i' does."

"That was very kind and," she hesitated for the right word, "thoughtful, Bertie. I shall cherish it."

"Ye must bury i'!" Bertie exclaimed. "Bury i' at thee threshold o' yer 'ouse!"

Agrippina started a moment at the old woman's

enthusiasm. "Yes, of course, I will do that. You are very kind to always be thinking of my safety."

"Ye and sir saved me," Bertie replied, her eyes filling with tears. "Ye saved me though ye didn' know me. Ye and sir are kind. More than anyone."

The old woman bowed her goodbyes and left Agrippina alone in the room holding the witch bottle, unsure of what to do with it.

"What is that?" Dr. Greystone asked as he reentered the room.

Agrippina opened her mouth to answer but thought better of it, shaking her head. "A small gift from Bertie. Something to protect us from," she hesitated, "witches."

"A witch bottle?" her uncle asked coming over and taking it from her. He walked over to the window to examine it better.

"Uh, yes, I believe that is what she said it was."

"Incredible. I have not seen one of these since your father and I did an investigation in Essex." He shook he bottle, pleased when he heard the nails scraping against the glass. "It appears to have a decent seal."

"We can all thank God for that," Agrippina muttered.

"How kind of her."

Mr. Mackland cleared his throat as he entered. "The driver says he is ready to go," he said almost regrettably.

"Of course! Drivers are always in a hurry to get on their way," Dr. Greystone said.

"Then, I suppose this is goodbye," Mr. Mackland ventured to say.

Agrippina said nothing. She didn't know what to say. Even if she did, she felt she could not say anything. She did not have to, however.

"May I write to you?" he asked her, causing her to blush.

Agrippina glanced at her uncle who wisely pretended not to hear as he left the room again, still examining the witch bottle as he did so.

"You are a certainly a person who is able to make his own decisions. I cannot see any reason physically stopping you from writing me," she finally surmised a little awkwardly.

Mr. Mackland chuckled. "Perhaps I worded my question incorrectly," he began. "What I meant to say is, would it please you if I wrote to you?"

At this, Agrippina's stomach twisted in excited knots and she stuttered. "Y—yes, I—I would not be opposed to having you as a correspondent." She looked away for a moment before she felt more in control of her emotions. "It would be nice to extend our acquaintance."

Mr. Mackland suppressed another laugh. "I suppose that is as favorable of an answer as I can expect." He smiled at her and held her gaze. "I believe I shall miss your matter-of-fact way of speaking."

Agrippina did not know how to reply having never received such a compliment before.

"I have never seen you so stumped for words," he continued with a smirk. "Have I flustered you? I hope you do not think me as too forward."

She shook her head. "No, I find you a perfect gentleman and I look forward to your letters."

He held out his arm which she took without hesitation allowing him to lead her outside. She turned to face him once more, taking in his features so she would not forget them. "Until we meet again, Miss Greystone," he whispered, sending a pleasant chill down her spine.

She gave a small curtsey and allowed him to hand her into the carriage, regretting a thousand different things as it pulled away and holding his gaze until he was no longer visible.

Dr. Greystone took a deep breath and let it out in a satisfied 'Aah!' "I think I much enjoyed it here," he proclaimed. "The air is clean; the land is beautiful. It was a nice escape from the bustling streets of Cambridge, do you not agree?"

Agrippina, never being able to find the joy in the little things, did not share her uncle's opinion. "I should have liked Blindburn more, I suppose, if it were not for the people."

He uncle laughed. "Bitter until the last, my dear," he playfully scolded. "You must learn how to enjoy yourself. You are too young to be so dreary all the time. Though you must admit we left a few interesting people behind." He lifted a knowing brow at her.

She chose to ignore it and pulled a book from her bag. "It certainly would have been interesting to have introduced Bertie to Abigail."

Dr. Greystone laughed. "I regret she stayed. She was a very entertaining woman, but that was not of whom I was speaking."

Agrippina lifted her gaze to meet her uncle's, but only for a moment.

"I was speaking of Mr. Mackland."

She nodded. "I know. And I do believe he is more of a gentleman than I gave him credit for upon first meeting him. I treated him abominably and he readily forgave me."

Dr. Greystone smiled. "What is there not to forgive?" he asked her.

Agrippina shrugged and sighed. "I do not know, perhaps the fact I accused him of not only murdering his sister but also four other women. That could not have felt very pleasant. I am sure I would have been quite angry if someone accused me of such a thing."

Her uncle smiled slyly. "I am sure most men would have

taken enough offense to not wish to see you again, but I have a feeling Mr. Mackland is not like other men. Especially in the attentions he gives you."

This time Agrippina blushed deeply. "You cannot suppose he would have feelings for me after all of that, uncle."

"I very well think that," he replied with a nod. "He is a sensible man and has forgiven you. And he has recognized that you are more than the mistakes you make. It will not be long before you hear from him. I guarantee it."

"Yes, but you think that of every man whom I come across. Besides, a long correspondence is too much trouble and he will certainly be too busy to write."

He nodded with a smile. "Trust me, my dear. You are worth the trouble."

Agrippina did not reply. She merely focused her attention out the window and watched as the outskirts of Blindburn slipped away behind them.

23

It was not long, as Dr. Greystone predicted, until Agrippina received a letter from Mr. Mackland. One arrived not a week after they returned to Cambridge. Her uncle had been pleased with himself to see how correct his assumption was and was even more pleased at another opportunity to tease his niece.

She, however, took her letter without a word and pretended to be indifferent at its existence though she burned to read it. It was not until her uncle hid himself away in his study did she finally relieve herself of her anticipation and tear open the seal.

She was pleased with his handwriting. Glad that he wrote so evenly and eloquently. She was hardly abashed at how she approved of him and was rather touched by his words. He asked her how her trip back home had been and told her how he had missed their conversations.

He even mentioned a trip to London sometime in the future and with a promise to call on her. The letter was proper and not presumptuous but she was not satisfied when she was done. She wished he had written more and even read and reread the letter multiple times to help satiate her feelings.

Her feelings, she thought to herself, were borderline ridiculous. She barely knew this man and here she was fawning over his written word to her. She sighed after reading it for the fourth time and was resolved to put it away when after half a minute she pulled the letter back out and read it again.

She smiled to herself, and allowed her stomach to flutter as she perused the lines where he complimented her. He said nothing of her beauty. No, any man could say she was beautiful. Instead, he focused on her pertinacity and intelligence. He congratulated her on her bravery at seeing the investigation into his sister's murder through even after she was attacked and was almost killed herself.

She smiled to herself as she stared at her letter, no longer having to read it as she already committed it to heart. After a moment, she stood from her seat and walked over to the writing desk by the window. She then took out a clean piece of paper and wrote back.

After months of correspondence, Agrippina grew used to waking up anxiously awaiting the mail. She would wait by the window for a letter and would always leave disappointed if she left before it came. Life for the most part returned to normal after they returned with her continuing to write lectures for her uncle and grade papers for Professor Hartley.

Life resumed its monotony and Agrippina found herself growing bored like she had never felt before. Other than the letters she received from Mr. Mackland, there was hardly anything exciting enough to distract her.

"Miss Greystone!" came a voice one afternoon as

Agrippina was walking along the river.

She turned to see Richard Maddox jogging up to her. "Mr. Maddox," she replied with a smile. "How are you?"

He smiled and bowed once he caught up to her. "I am quite well. Thank you. I have missed seeing you, however, though I am sure you have not noticed my absence."

"You are mistaken. My uncle's class has been a lot quieter recently," she jested dryly. "Your absence could have been the only reason."

He chuckled. "You always know how to make a man feel good about himself."

"Ah, it is my life's mission, Mr. Maddox. I am glad to see I am accomplishing it."

He smiled again, but more softly. "I heard around campus about your adventures up north."

She nodded.

"I heard you solved a murder."

She nodded again. "Nine murders, if we are being exact, with the help of my uncle."

He shook his head. "I heard you did most of the work."

"Have you been talking to my uncle, then?"

He laughed. "He told me so himself that he merely guided you when necessary but you are the one that did the hard labor."

"That was a little bit of an exaggeration. My uncle is too kind and you should know by now that he often highlights my good qualities while ignoring my bad ones."

"Does Miss Greystone have any bad qualities?" He smirked.

She laughed through her nose.

There was a brief silence broken by Mr. Maddox clearing his throat.

"The reason I sought you out here, Miss Greystone, is

because I might need some help myself."

She frowned. "What do you mean?"

"Well, I am from Essex, as you know."

She nodded. "Yes, I remember."

"And I am sure you remember my sudden departure from Cambridge after a letter from my sister?"

Again, she nodded. "Yes, it was the night of the gathering at the Hills."

He paused briefly. "Well, if you did not know, Essex is witch country."

Agrippina furrowed her brows a moment in confusion. "Witch country?" she repeated. "I was not aware something of that nature existed."

He nodded. "Yes, and my absence at Cambridge has something to do with that very issue."

Agrippina blinked at him. "With witches?"

He let out a huff. "Yes," he replied without any explanation.

"Mr. Maddox, I understand you do not tend to take life seriously, but I do. I do not need you to play jokes on me while I am trying to enjoy a few moments' peace before I resume my duties for the rest of the day."

He blinked at her, confused by her reaction. "Miss Greystone, I, by no means, am playing a joke on you. Believe it or not, I respect you too much to do so. What I am telling you is the truth. Essex is known for its witches and very recently there have been some rather," he stopped for a moment as he thought of what he wanted to say, "disturbing events occurring there."

She regarded him for a moment without response.

"Now, I know you are a sensible woman and tend to look at things logically without jumping to conclusions which is why I am here asking for your help."

Agrippina was taken aback. "My help?"

He nodded. "Yes. There have been some sort of mysterious happenings going on in Halstead, a town not far from my uncle's estate."

"The uncle you are to inherit from?"

"Yes, and he is concerned for the locals," he continued. "Particularly, some of the farmers." He sighed. "Anyway, none of the local authorities know what to do, and when I heard about your success in Blindburn, I could not think of anyone else to go to for help."

Agrippina stood a little straighter after that comment and suppressed a triumphant smirk. "Yes, well, I would need to talk to my uncle, of course, and check my availability."

They turned together to return to campus.

"I am rather intrigued by these 'disturbing events' though," she went on. "Might you be able to elaborate?"

Agrippina allowed him to talk all the while planning out her next adventure.

THE END